"I want the truth," he growled.

The pale eyes pleaded with him.

"I want to tell you, Kal," she whispered, what little color there was in her face draining from it. "But now?"

"Now!" he said, listening to the voice in his head that was suggesting the woman was up to something and ignoring common sense, which reminded him that the hospital needed her expertise and he shouldn't be antagonizing her.

But she was antagonizing him just by being here—making him want to touch her, to take her in his arms and hold her, remembering her body, kiss her, remembering her lips....

POSH DOCS

Dedicated, daring and devastatingly handsome—these doctors are guaranteed to raise your temperature!

Meet the doctors who are
the best in the business....

Whether they're saving lives in the hospital,
or romancing in the bedroom, they
always get pulses racing!

SHEIKH SURGEON

MEREDITH WEBBER

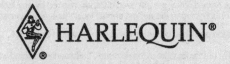

TORONTO • NEW YORK • LONDON
AMSTERDAM • PARIS • SYDNEY • HAMBURG
STOCKHOLM • ATHENS • TOKYO • MILAN • MADRID
PRAGUE • WARSAW • BUDAPEST • AUCKLAND

ISBN-13: 978-0-373-82048-1
ISBN-10:   0-373-82048-8

SHEIKH SURGEON

First North American Publication 2006.

Copyright © 2006 by Meredith Webber.

All rights reserved. Except for use in any review, the reproduction or utilization of this work in whole or in part in any form by any electronic, mechanical or other means, now known or hereafter invented, including xerography, photocopying and recording, or in any information storage or retrieval system, is forbidden without the written permission of the publisher, Harlequin Enterprises Limited, 225 Duncan Mill Road, Don Mills, Ontario, Canada M3B 3K9.

All characters in this book have no existence outside the imagination of the author and have no relation whatsoever to anyone bearing the same name or names. They are not even distantly inspired by any individual known or unknown to the author, and all incidents are pure invention.

This edition published by arrangement with Harlequin Books S.A.

® and TM are trademarks of the publisher. Trademarks indicated with ® are registered in the United States Patent and Trademark Office, the Canadian Trade Marks Office and in other countries.

www.eHarlequin.com

Printed in U.S.A.

SHEIKH
SURGEON

CHAPTER ONE

KAL watched the bird spiral upwards, riding the desert thermals higher and higher until it was a black speck against the impossibly blue sky. The bird's flight lifted his spirit until it seemed his soul soared with it, released from the imprisonment of his body. Only here, alone in an endless sea of sand, did he experience the lightness of spirit that was close to happiness.

As close as he would ever come…

Suddenly, the black speck dropped like a stone, down and down and down, wings tucked back to add destructive power to the speeding descent. It disappeared from sight behind a sand dune, and Kal whistled then held out his arm for the bird's return.

It had missed its kill and he wasn't sorry—he had food enough for himself and the bird. But the falcon's failure reminded him how long it had been since he'd spent time with his birds—flying them and training them. His men exercised them regularly, but they didn't have the same touch and the birds knew it.

But what was more important? Training falcons the way his ancestors had for thousands of years, or bringing modern medicine to his country—providing the best medical services for his people?

He slipped the bird's hood over its head and set it on a stand, his hand lingering on the shiny dark feathers, feeling a tight bond with this living creature that could fly so freely, yet returned willingly to its captivity. Just as he would return to the hospital, for to do anything else would be unthinkable.

But not until tomorrow…

He walked back across a sand hill to where he'd left his big four-wheel-drive, and brought out a bundle of sticks. He'd build a fire and camp out beneath the stars—forget the world he was escaping, if only for a night. But though the stars shone like a scattering of bright diamonds in the velvety night sky, and the wind across the desert sands soothed him with its song, he couldn't recapture the lightness he'd felt as he'd watched the bird soar, and his mood turned deep and heavy—his soul now a weighted stone within him.

The plane dropped beneath the clouds and there, spreading to the horizon, were the desert sands, just as Kal had described them—a golden sea, with wave upon wave of wind-sculpted dunes. Kal had spoken of their beauty, but the longing in his voice when he'd mentioned the desert had told Nell more than words ever could have. The man she'd loved had loved this arid country with a bone-deep passion bred into him over the thousands of years his ancestors had roamed those sands.

Now, seeing them for the first time, Nell clasped her hands tightly together, the photo of Patrick—Patrick with hair—before the cancer—squashed between them. It was like a talisman, this photo, and she'd held it tightly throughout the twelve-hour flight, so now the outer plastic cover was sticky with her worrying and a crease was developing across her son's finely aquiline nose.

Patrick was well—she'd phoned home twice from the plane, the first time because she'd been intrigued to find all she had to do was swipe her credit card in the receiver then dial, and the second time to hear Patrick's voice one more time before they landed.

This remission would last. She had to be as positive as he was. Yet here she was about to land in a foreign country, just in case being positive wasn't good enough.

Just in case…

'Safely down,' the comfortably plump woman beside her said, and Nell registered the jolt she'd felt and opened her eyes. The woman and her husband had been kind and undemanding travelling companions, so Nell smiled at them and wished them all the best for the rest of their journey.

They knew part of her story—the part where she was travelling to this desert country to demonstrate the use of spray-on skin for burns victims. It was something that had been developed in the burns unit where she worked and fate had played into her hands when the hospital here had requested information on the innovative technique for their new burns unit and had asked if perhaps someone would come and demonstrate it.

A month, that's all Nell had—to both explain the treatment to the staff at the hospital and to find Patrick's father. To somehow tell him, at the risk of her own hard-won emotional security, that he had a son—a son who might, one day soon, need his help and the help of his people…

She closed her eyes again—the magnitude of *that* particular exercise all but overwhelming her. It would be all right, she promised herself as the plane taxied towards the low, well-lit terminal. It *had* to be all right!

But once out of the safety of the plane, nerves began gnawing at Nell's stomach. Through passport control—purpose of visit to this desert kingdom, business—and customs—no, nothing to declare—the gnawing grew stronger and stronger until she wondered if people could develop stomach ulcers in such a short time.

A door at the far end of the customs hall spilled her out into a wide foyer, crowded with people clamouring for a glimpse of their returning loved ones. And at the back of the crowd, a small sign held aloft. DR WARREN was all it said, but the woman in the headscarf who held it was smiling so warmly Nell felt the panic in her stomach ease.

'I'm Nell Warren,' she said, pushing through the crowd and holding out her hand to the smiling woman.

'Yasmeen,' the woman offered, shaking Nell's hand and drawing her further from the jostling crowd. Then a screeching, rending, tearing noise, so loud and fearsome it conjured up images of other worlds, rent the air, and people began to scream and scream so when the sirens started, they were like a continuation of the high-pitched sounds of terror.

'Something has gone wrong.' Yasmeen stated the obvious, but she was already moving with a purpose. 'All hospital staff take part in simulated airport emergencies,' she said over her shoulder. 'I must go. You can stay here and wait.'

'If it's an emergency, the more hands you have the better,' Nell told her, dropping her small suitcase beside a pillar and hurrying after the woman through a crowd that was now in full panic mode despite what were probably reassurances echoing from the public-address system.

Ducking and weaving, they finally reached a deserted corridor on the ground floor, and Yasmeen pushed through a door into a large room, glass windows on the far side of which reflected the angry red glow of a fierce fire. Going towards the windows, Nell saw the fire engines racing across the tarmac, some units already in place, sending streams of snow-like foam onto the angry conflagration.

Yasmeen was murmuring to herself—a prayer, Nell guessed, for her own heart was praying for whoever was trapped in the burning plane. The door behind them opened and more people swept in, some wheeling trolleys, others carrying first-aid equipment. Two ambulances pulled up outside, the public-address system issued what had to be instructions, and Nell felt the tension build as emergency crews awaited the order to move.

'We will wait here and treat the injured as they are brought in,' Yasmeen said to Nell. 'As the first doctors on the scene, we must do what we can. The hospital will be on full alert by now and more ambulances will be here shortly. The worst cases we'll send straight to the hospital where emergency teams will have more facilities to treat them.'

Nell looked at the burning aircraft and wondered if they would have any patients to treat. Surely no one could escape so fierce a fire.

'Do you know what happened?'

Yasmeen shook her head.

'From what people are saying around me, it seems the plane was coming in to land—praise be it wasn't your plane—when it skidded on the runway. Maybe the wheels didn't lock, or some oil made it skid. It slewed off sideways, hit a stationary plane, and then burst into flames.'

Nell shook her head, imagining the horror of those on board. How many had there been? She couldn't tell how big the burning plane was, but her flight had carried over four hundred people.

'Look!' Yasmeen grabbed her arm, and there, black against the leaping red and orange flames, were small figures, fleeing across the tarmac.

'So some have survived,' Nell murmured, watching as airport vehicles stopped by the small figures, collecting them, then speeding towards the room where she and Yasmeen waited with the other emergency staff.

It was her last rational thought for some hours. The first victims had been lucky—not badly burned—so the job was to clean the wounds and dress them, to wrap blankets around shaking shoulders and treat them for shock. But as the room filled with the less badly injured, the scene of operations moved outside onto the tarmac, where arc lights lit a scene from hell.

'Cover wounds with clean dry cloth, intubate if their airways seem undamaged—if there are no burns on their face or throat—but otherwise provide oxygen through a mask. Remember a lot will have lung damage from inhaling the heat and smoke. Get fluids flowing in,' Nell said to Yasmeen, who had hesitated beside her as the more seriously injured began to arrive. 'Raise the injured parts and treat for shock, don't attempt to treat the burns, don't peel off clothes, don't puncture blisters, don't raise their heads as it could compromise their airways,' Nell added, aware she probably had more experience in burns first aid than the other doctor. 'Tell the other people here to do the same. Would you like me to do the triage? Sending the worst cases to hospital first?'

Yasmeen nodded and though Nell could feel the other woman shaking beside her, Yasmeen pulled herself together and gave orders in a crisp clear voice.

Mobile medical supply vans had appeared from nowhere, the sides of the vans opening up to reveal an abundance of equipment. As she checked patients and tagged them in order of the severity of their injuries, Nell marvelled at the organisational set-up of the airport that it had these vans on standby.

She worked as if controlled from somewhere outside herself, checking, treating, passing patients on, until at last more and more of the bodies being pulled from the plane were already dead and the grim task of handling them could be turned over to someone else.

'Come on,' she said to Yasmeen. 'We'll be needed at the hospital.'

The other woman's face was black with soot and grime from the clothes of the patients they'd treated, and Nell guessed her own was just as bad, but Yasmeen's smile lit up her darkened face and she shook her head at Nell's suggestion.

'You're a guest here and you've already done enough to help,' she protested. 'I will take you to the quarters we've arranged for you where you can clean up and rest.'

Then it was Nell's turn to shake *her* head.

'No way! This is what I do, Yasmeen! I'm a specialist burns doctor. How many of them does your hospital have? I also know the uses of the spray-on skin—that's why I'm here, remember. Take me to the hospital. I can help in either your emergency room or wherever else I'm needed.'

She smiled at her new friend.

'I'll clean up first,' she promised.

Yasmeen smiled again, then led the way back through the airport and out the other side to where cars jammed the roads, news of the accident having sent panicking relations racing to the airport.

'It's a gridlock. We'll never get away. Perhaps we should go back and hitch a ride with an ambulance,' Nell suggested, but a clattering noise drowned out the words and she looked up to see a helicopter descending towards the far side of the terminal building.

'Come on—that's the best ride for us. The chief's own personal helicopter. He's been talking about getting one for the hospital, but until it happens, he's willing to use his own for emergencies.'

Yasmeen grabbed Nell's arm and hurried her back the way they'd come.

'I was wondering why he hadn't turned up earlier, then remembered he'd taken some rare time off and had probably gone out to the desert.'

Yasmeen was talking of this 'chief' with a mixture of respect and affection as she led the way through the milling crowds, and from the words she used—'chief' in particular—and her accented English, Nell guessed she'd trained, for a time at least, in the United States.

'This chief? Is he a department head? Or the hospital CEO?' Nell asked, and Yasmeen turned to flash another smile her way.

'Chief surgeon, head of the hospital, and also a member of our ruling family. Khalil al Kalada is a great man who was not only born to greatness but has lived up to the finest of his family's traditions.'

Khalil al Kalada.

The words seemed to come from a great distance,

echoing through space, closer and closer until they hammered like drumbeats in Nell's head.

Cold fear clutched at her heart while panic spread through her body. Not yet, her mind yelled. I'm not ready yet! But though her feet faltered Yasmeen urged her on, racing her headlong towards a meeting with the man she'd come so far to find.

As Kal brought the helicopter down, he saw the wreckage of the still smouldering plane in the distance, his father's helicopter parked a little to one side of it, but the medical action would be where the arc lights lit up a makeshift emergency room.

Still cursing the fact he'd taken his vehicle, not the chopper, out to the desert so his response time to the emergency call had been slow, he hovered for a moment, taking in the traffic jam beyond the terminal building, picking out the flashing red lights of ambulances and other emergency vehicles stuck in a seemingly impossible tangle of cars. Police vehicles were clearing the road, forcing cars to the verges so ambulances could get through. It was making the tangle of civilian traffic worse, but at least the ambulances were moving.

His father's pilot would be at the controls of the helicopter on the ground, awaiting orders. Kal radioed him, telling him to take off and offer assistance to the police vehicles, advising clear routes and using a loudhailer to get non-essential vehicles off the road. He'd have liked to have called police headquarters as well and suggest they arrest any non-emergency personnel on the roads, but that might be a little extreme…

A light touch on the controls brought him lower. He'd

check the situation on the ground then head straight back
to the hospital. By now a call would have gone out to all
staff, asking them to report for duty. The facilities would
be stretched to the limit—he'd have to contact nearby
states and ask if they could take patients. Could some be
airlifted to hospitals further afield? His father's private
plane had as much medical equipment as a state-of-the art
emergency room, while his family's business interests
were spread like tentacles throughout the world. There'd
be contacts who'd smooth the way for the repatriation of
foreign patients…

He landed in the darkness beyond the arc lights, left
the cabin and ran, bent low to dodge the slowing rotors,
towards the centre of the activity. As ever, some people
stopped work to nod or make a tentative bow towards
him, unable to prevent themselves offering this small
acknowledgement, but a tall man in smoke-blackened
robes stepped forward to greet him with a handshake.

'I'm head of airport security, Highness,' the man said,
giving his name as he grasped Kal's hand. 'All we know is
that the plane skidded off the runway, hit a stationary plane
and burst into flames. The worst cases are on their way to
hospital, minor injuries and people still shocked are being
treated by our staff inside the building, and now we are
getting ready to transport those deceased to the mortuary.'

He waved his hand towards a line of shrouded bodies.

'So many dead!' Kal murmured, pain for the waste of
life biting into him even while he accepted the deaths as
God's will.

'More would be dead but for the doctors from your
hospital who were here on hand to help the injured and
tell my staff exactly how to treat them.'

The man paused then added, 'More will die, Excellency. Many on the way to hospital are very badly burnt.'

'Then I must go—they'll need me there,' Kal told him. He'd have liked to have added that he didn't need the royal terms of address—didn't use them himself—but he sensed the man needed the formality and ritual—needed to know some things didn't change and that while a member of the ruling family was present, all would be taken care of.

But as Kal turned back towards the helicopter, a voice called his name, and he turned to see two women hurrying towards him.

'Sir, Yasmeen—I'm Yasmeen Assanti, Ward Six. I was here, collecting the woman from Australia who was coming to show us the spray-on skin. I told her not to help but she knows burns better than I do. She's been like an angel of mercy, sir. We'd have lost more people without her.'

She turned, apparently to introduce the 'angel of mercy', but the second woman was now crouched on the ground, holding a shroud high and peering at the person lying beneath it.

'He's alive!' she called, her voice so hoarse it came out like a croak.

Kal dashed towards her, kneeling on the other side, calling for lights to be directed on the patient, checking the man who'd been left for dead.

'Get him into my helicopter,' he yelled, beckoning to two men who were lifting bodies into the mortuary van. 'Yasmeen, get fluids and something clean to cover him. You…' He glanced at the woman across the stretcher. 'Stay with him. Do what you can.'

She nodded, her hands still busy checking the patient, feeling for first a radial then a carotid pulse.

'Oxygen, too, Yasmeen,' she said, lifting her head briefly so Kal had an impression of pale eyes in a blackened face. But it was her voice, although raspy with the smoke and soot she'd inhaled, that sent a shiver down his spine, and out of nowhere came an expression he'd heard while studying in Australia—something about a ghost walking over a grave.

He stepped back to make room for Yasmeen, then two men were lifting the stretcher, and the stranger was walking beside it, holding an oxygen mask in one hand, just above the injured man's nose, and the heavy oxygen bottle in her other hand.

Kal raced ahead of them to open the doors of the helicopter and prepare it to receive the stretcher, then, after giving orders to the men about how to strap it into place, he climbed forward into the pilot's seat and prepared to take off, checking with Air Traffic Control that he was cleared to take off.

Above them planes would be circling, unable to land. Most would be diverted to nearby airports, or turned back if they were on short flights. He had no doubt one of his brothers would be in the control tower, making sure everything was being done efficiently up there, while another brother would be handling questions from the media as news of the disaster spread beyond the narrow confines of his country.

But as the little helicopter rose easily into the air, staying below the level of the circling planes, he turned to look back into the cabin, where a dirty, dishevelled woman knelt beside an injured man.

It couldn't be...

'I can't get a tube in,' Nell muttered to Yasmeen. 'His

airway's compromised. Hold the mask just slightly above his mouth and nose so it doesn't stick to his burnt skin. I've got pure oxygen flowing out so whatever he manages to breathe in— No! Damn! He's not breathing by himself at all now. This is what can happen—suddenly his airway collapses altogether or oedema closes it.'

She switched tubes so she could bag the man, forcing air into his lungs while Yasmeen held the mask, but the man's chest failed to move.

'He needs a tracheostomy so we can insert a tube into his trachea, but because of the oedema and because the lungs might have suffered major damage, the pressure of pumped oxygen could...'

She was thinking out loud, but knew the tracheostomy was the only way to go, although it carried severe risks for burns patients. Yasmeen had brought a medical kit out to the helicopter, and Nell found a packaged scalpel and another package with tubing in it.

Yasmeen touched her hand.

'Do it,' she said, but the man's clothing had burnt to the skin on his neck and Nell's fingers faltered as she sought the tracheal rings through which she could plunge the scalpel.

In the end she took a chance on the position and was relieved to hear a release of air. Once a small tube was in place to keep the gap open, she saw the man's chest rise and fall.

He was breathing by himself!

She took a deep breath herself, then Yasmeen leaned close to talk above the noise.

'That's the hospital up ahead. We'll land on the roof. Strap into a seat.'

And leave this man who'd been left for dead once already?

'I'll hang on tightly,' Nell told Yasmeen, taking the oxygen mask from the other doctor and holding it close to the tracheostomy tube, still worrying about the extent of lung damage her patient might be suffering and whether too much oxygen would exacerbate it. Lungs were delicate—pressure could burst them. Inhaled heat and particles of noxious gas would already have damaged the fine tissues...

At least worrying about her patient stopped her worrying about the man flying the helicopter. His glance had done no more than pass over her earlier, and for that she was sincerely thankful.

OK, she had to talk to Kal some time—that was why she'd come. But exhausted from travel, shaken by the emergency and covered with soot and ash? Hardly!

The little craft touched down lightly, then he was there again, kneeling right beside her.

'A tracheostomy on a burns patient—contraindicated surely,' he said, his voice stern with disapproval.

'He wasn't breathing and we couldn't force air into his lungs,' Yasmeen said. 'Dr Warren tried. She tried everything before she resorted to cutting him.'

The fluid catheter was leaking along the patient's arm and Nell's head was bent, trying to find a new site, while this conversation took place. It was a measure of her involvement with the injured man—of her determination to keep him alive—that she could stay focussed on what she was doing, aware of Kal only on the periphery of her conscious mind.

Or maybe her concentration was a coping mechanism.

She felt the slight pop as the needle entered a vein and, holding the catheter in place, she reached with her free hand for tape. Long slim fingers pressed what she needed into her hand—not Yasmeen's fingers, which were blunt and slightly chubby. The touch was cool—impersonal— and though her conscious mind had lost the battle to keep Kal at bay and her body was quaking with an apprehensive dread, she calmly taped the catheter into place and reattached the drip tube.

'We can move him now,' she said, keeping her back to the man who knelt beside her, looking instead towards the group of people gathered at the open door of the helicopter.

'Dr Warren?'

Kal's voice, familiar enough to send shivers up her spine although her name was unfamiliar on his lips.

'I'll go with the patient,' she said, fussing with the tube, battling for emotional control. Deliberately rude, but so tense she feared she'd shatter into a million pieces if she turned to face Kal now.

Then an image of Patrick's face rose up in her mind. She couldn't risk getting off on the wrong foot with Kal.

Her heart hammered with panic, a thousand butterflies fluttered inside her, and her knees and fingers trembled with uncertainty, and fear, and dread, and some other emotion she didn't want to think about. But she was a grown woman, with a son who needed help, so she lifted her head, met his eyes, forced a facsimile of a smile to her lips, and said, 'Hello, Kal.'

But before he could reply the man on the stretcher gave a convulsive lurch and became the focus of her attention once again. She leant across him, holding him still, checking that the incision she'd made in his throat was still open.

'Yasmeen?' The woman had come to the opposite side of the stretcher as it was lifted, and Nell spoke across the patient. 'Do many of your staff speak English? Will the nurses understand me if I ask for things?'

'Yasmeen will stay with you to translate until a nurse who speaks English can be found. It shouldn't take long as most of our staff are bilingual.'

So much for not getting off on the wrong foot. His voice would have frozen fire!

He delivered this reply then strode away, a stranger in a smoke-grimed white robe, pulling off his headdress, grabbing scrubs from a trolley as he passed, turning from the desert chieftain she'd seen emerge from the helicopter into a doctor once again.

Why, after fourteen years would she turn up in his country?

Coincidence?

He didn't think so.

But he couldn't think of any reason for her to have come. She'd assume he was still married so it couldn't have been some mid-life crisis to reclaim her youth.

Could it?

No, not Nell, who was sensible and pragmatic and who'd understood his position from the start.

Besides, she was married, too—her name was Warren, not Roberts—though she wore no rings...

Kal shook his head as he ducked into a side room and pulled off his robe, seeing sand from the desert spill on the floor, staring at the last reminder of his hours of freedom as he tried to get his head back on track. He pulled on the loose scrubs. He was a doctor again—a doctor with a huge emergency in his hospital and a strange feeling in the pit of his stomach. No way could he let his thinking be distracted by Nell's presence in his hospital. If anything, he should be grateful—the Dr Warren he'd expected was a burns expert and if ever one was needed, it was now.

Dr Warren!

She must *have married...*

Why ever wouldn't she?

He had.

But pointing this out to himself didn't make him feel any better about Nell marrying, though he knew it was irrational to be thinking about Nell at all—let alone about her marital status...

'We've sixty-two victims in the ER so far.' Lalla el Wafa, his A and E nurse-manager, met him as he came out of the elevator on the ground floor. 'The doctors on duty haven't been able to do more than check their status, make sure their airways are patent and that they're getting fluids and electrolytes.'

'We take one patient at a time and do what we can. What we don't do is panic,' Kal told her.

They'd paused in the passageway and now had to stand against the wall to allow the wardsmen wheeling the injured man Kal had transported to pass. Nell was still beside him, bending over him to hold a mask close to the tube in his throat.

Was she worried about lung damage that she hadn't attached the tube directly to the oxygen tank? He must ask her later. Since the explosion at an oil well three months ago that had prompted him to open a burns unit at the hospital, he'd been reading up on treatment of burns victims. It had changed so much since his training days when he'd dealt with an occasional burn in ER, and he still didn't know as much as he needed to know. Neither had he been able to find a suitable specialist doctor to employ as head of the unit.

Maybe he could persuade Nell to stay.

Are you going mental?

The group disappeared through the doors at the end of the corridor, but Kal still stared in that direction. As the doors had slid open Nell had lifted her head to speak to Yasmeen and he'd noticed the clean-cut profile, with a long straight nose.

A nose Nell Roberts had always thought far too long for her to ever be considered beautiful…

A nose he'd kissed a thousand times…

CHAPTER TWO

HE CAUGHT up with Nell as the man was wheeled into a curtained alcove, but the sight of sixty-two—no, sixty-three now—patients in the ER stopped him following her—*and* demanding answers to all the questions in his head. Blackened, blistered, wailing with pain, the injured lay against the wall, and were slumped on chairs, while those tagged more urgent were on trolleys, which were in lines four or five deep.

'Have they been sorted into priorities?' he asked Lalla, who had followed him and was still hovering by his side.

'Someone at the airport toe-tagged them and we're working off that classification.'

Kal guessed who the someone was. He looked at the patients lying on makeshift stretchers along the far wall—tagged less urgent but they'd be in pain, and would be suffering shock. A young doctor was yelling for more fluids, while another was lifting an injured man in his arms, obviously desperate to get him to a treatment room, but they were all full, with staff rushing in all directions—a scene from hell.

He and his staff could handle burns cases—they had

before and they knew the current emergency procedures—but they usually handled one person coming in
with burns—six with the oil fire. Not sixty-three, a lot of
them foreign, and a lot of them so severely burned he
wondered if they'd live.

'Kal, I don't want to be telling you your business, but
you have to do this systematically.' Nell emerged from
the curtained alcove and stopped in front of him, deliver-
ing this opening foray without a hint of apology in her
voice. 'Staff should calculate the total body surface area
burned using the rule of nine. Any patient with more than
twenty per cent TBSA should be given fluids—Ringer's
lactate for the first twenty-four hours. We'll work out
electrolyte balance later. They should be catheterised and
their fluid output measured. Ideally it should be evaluat-
ed for haemoglobin, which would show a breakdown in
red blood cells and could lead to kidney failure. At the
first sign of red blood cell breakdown, they'll need a diu-
retic to clear the fluid faster to protect the kidneys.'

Kal stared at the woman standing in front of him, telling him what to do, as if this was the most natural thing
in the world. Did she feel nothing of the emotional chaos
he was suffering? Or was she just far more capable of
separating her emotional self from her practical one?

'Tell them to dress the wounds with whatever sterile
dressings you have available—we've time later to do
excisions and skin grafts and fancy stuff. That can wait at
least twenty-four hours post-burn—even up to five days
if necessary—but right now we have to stop fluid loss
through bleeding or wound seepage and stabilise the
patients as best we can.'

'Pain relief?' he asked, as the crying, wailing and

moaning broke through the turmoil in his mind. Of course Nell should be telling him what to do—it was her field of expertise. And, of course, he too could separate his emotional self from his practical one—hadn't he been doing it for years?

'Morphine's the best. IV. They'll all be getting fluids anyway. Then I need someone—you, probably, as Yasmeen says you're a surgeon—to check the wounds for bands of eschar—circumferential burns on the chest or extremities.'

'Cut through them?' Kal asked, pleased to find he was able to talk to the suddenly reappeared Nell as if she was just another doctor.

His body didn't think she was just another doctor, though why his body should be responding to anything but the medical emergency he had no idea.

She nodded.

'You won't need anaesthetic. It only happens in third-degree burns and the nerve endings in the skin have all been destroyed so it doesn't hurt the patient, but you'll be opening up more surface area to infection, so a topical antibiotic and a clean dressing should be applied.'

'Will one cut suffice?'

The pale eyes studied him, a frown gathering between her neatly arched brows.

Frown lines—she's got frown lines!

'It usually does, but you'll be able to tell if one cut's enough. With extremities—eschar on the arms or legs— you'll get a pulse in the wrist or ankle once you're done. With chest constriction, you might need two cuts—one midclavicular and one transverse. You'll see the chest rise and fall once it's free.'

Yasmeen called to her and she turned away—then swung back to call after Kal, 'Don't tie off bleeders on the limbs immediately. Let them bleed three to five minutes to release pressure, but holding the extremity above heart level. Then tie them off or coagulate. And tetanus prophylaxis—conscious patients will be able to tell you their tetanus status. And nil by mouth on all of them— paralytic ileus.'

Kal nodded, knowing that, but also knowing she was right to remind him—to remind them all—of the basic treatment. One burns patient coming in would be treated quickly and efficiently, with all these reminders Nell had issued in the forefront of the ER doctor's mind, but, faced with so many patients, it would be easy for a doctor, anxious to do everything for everyone, to forget something of the basics.

Kal moved away, aware of Nell going not to the man they'd airlifted to hospital, but to check a very small patient on a trolley by the far wall. Yasmeen was bent over the trolley, talking anxiously to Nell, but Nell's frown told Kal it was too late. That he was looking at the first of the hospital casualties.

'Even if we could have saved him,' Nell told Yasmeen, 'he wouldn't have survived very long. Look at his little body—can you see a bit of it that isn't burned? Adults with more than sixty per cent burns to their bodies have little chance of survival, so what hope would this tiny soul have had?'

She put her arm around Yasmeen's shoulders and led her away, reminding her they had living patients to tend. Reminding herself of the same thing. Her mind argued that she shouldn't have spoken to Kal as she had, giving orders, but although all ER doctors knew the routine for treating burns patients, she'd been in emergency situations before and was aware that the sheer volume of patients at a time like this threw normal thinking into disarray.

She moved on to the man who'd been left for dead, catheterised him then sent a urine sample to the lab for testing, checked the oxygen level in his blood—still too low—fiddled with the oxygen valve to produce more flow, then knew she had to move on. There were too many patients for her to be spending time with one man.

'You've always got to be aware of carbon monoxide poisoning with burn victims,' she explained to a young doctor who seemed mesmerised by a patient with the tell-tale cherry-red colouring. 'The blood carries carbon monoxide far more easily than it carries oxygen—for some reason haemoglobin has an affinity with the carbon monoxide molecules. So, as well as the patient breathing in the deadly fumes, the blood's too busy shunting the wrong gas around the body to be bothered with oxygen.'

'Is that why the patient's unconscious? Carbon monoxide poisoning rather than burns?'

Nell looked at the patient, reassessing the percentage of injured body surface area.

'Most probably. Pump one hundred per cent oxygen into him, but watch for a change in his level of consciousness. Do you have a hyperbaric chamber?'

The young doctor looked puzzled. 'Like we use for divers with the bends?'

Nell nodded.

'Yes. We have a lot of tourists coming here to dive, so we've always had one in the hospital.'

'Well, if he's still unconscious in, say, an hour, we

should put him in there. The situation is similar to someone with the bends. We need to get the carbon monoxide out of his blood using pressure, then force oxygen in.'

She glanced up from writing this advice on the chart to see Kal had joined them.

'We've others affected by carbon monoxide. I'll make sure all the staff know to check the level of consciousness of their patients.'

He disappeared again, but from time to time, as she worked, Nell was aware of him nearby. Sometimes he'd ask a question or direct her to a particular patient.

Nell moved among the doctors and nurses fighting for the lives of these badly injured people, aware of how different this type of doctoring was. No one was taking records of past illnesses, and in a lot of cases they didn't know the patient's name or nationality. It was enough to know a human being in terrible distress lay on the stretcher in front of them, and to do everything possible, firstly to save that person's life then to ease their pain and keep infection at bay.

A couple of times Yasmeen dragged her away to a small sitting room, where exhausted staff sat silently as they refuelled on coffee and biscuits. Sandwiches appeared and were eaten on the run, staff aware they had to eat but their minds always on the patients.

At some stage Kal walked past and she remembered something else that needed checking.

'Eschar on joints, too,' she said to him. 'Sometimes you need to cut along the outer surface of a limb at wrist, elbow, knee or ankle joint. Mobility is a huge problem for burns victims later, and sometimes we can prevent problems by releasing burnt tissue early. Again, the wounds will bleed a lot but cauterise them this time.'

Kal nodded and walked away, and Nell knew every patient in ER would be checked for any burnt tissue that might be constricting movement of a limb.

Uncountable hours later, the scene in the ER looked less like a vision of hell, though torn wrappings from dressings and instruments still lay ankle deep on the floor. They had transferred fourteen critically injured patients to the new burns unit, two of these to the burns ICU, and another eleven were in wards throughout the hospital. Twenty-one less badly injured had been treated and either sent home or put up in hotels, and another ten, who were members of a football team from a neighbouring country, had been flown home in the ruler's private plane, to be treated at the main hospital in their capital city.

The small child had been the first of six patients they hadn't been able to save and Nell was still in the ER, still fighting for the life of the man who'd been left for dead.

'Let someone take him up to the ward,' Yasmeen pleaded, her face cleaned of soot but now grey with exhaustion. 'We can make room for him there and the nurses are fresh—they can watch him for you.'

'I won't move him till he's stable,' Nell muttered, checking again on the test results she'd just got from the lab. 'His acid base status is all over the place. It *has* to be to do with inhalation injury, although his lungs show clear on the X-ray. He's not pink so it's not carbon monoxide, and with a tube in place it can't be swelling to his lower trachea, although that rarely happens because the vocal cords effectively stop heat going further.'

Once again she found herself thinking out loud, but if she expected help from Yasmeen she was disappointed. The other doctor simply repeated her advice that Nell should hand the patient over and get some rest.

'But—' she began, then another voice cut in.

'We're taking him up to the ward.'

Nell glanced up from the infuriating puzzle that was this patient to see Kal standing in the opening of the curtained-off treatment room, and though his statement had been an order, not a suggestion, she had to argue.

'He shouldn't be moved.'

'He has to be moved,' Kal said firmly. 'You've done all you can and you're so close to exhaustion you could make the mistake that kills him.'

Shocked by his blunt words, Nell opened her mouth to continue her argument, then read the implacability on his face and closed it again.

'Yasmeen,' Kal continued smoothly, 'I'll find someone to go with him and make sure he has a nurse to watch him. You go home and get some rest. I'll see Dr Warren to her quarters as soon as I've arranged the transfer.'

Nell opened her mouth again, this time to protest that she could find her own way—a protest so stupid it was just as well no sound came out. Not that Kal would have heard. He'd disappeared.

'Come on,' Kal said roughly, returning minutes later. He took her arm and guided her firmly away. 'You're dead on your feet.'

Realising resistance was futile, Nell plodded along

beside him, her legs apparently understanding what he'd said, as they became so heavy she could barely lift them.

Beside her, Kal muttered words that seeped dimly into her consciousness—angry words from the tone.

Was he telling her she was a fool? He used to tell her that when she meekly accepted the worst shifts during in-hospital training stints. Or when she'd lent her notes to friends who'd skipped lectures.

'You're smiling?'

His voice was so incredulous she couldn't stop her smile from widening.

'It must be tiredness because I rarely think about the past, but I was remembering how you used to call me a fool,' she said, turning to face him and looking into his eyes for the first time, scanning his face for similarities and differences, seeking something of the serious young man she'd loved to distraction in the tired, hard, angry, unshaven face.

'A long time ago,' she added quietly, then, because the young man *was* there and because her heart told her she *still* loved him, she turned away before he could read it in her eyes and her quest became more complicated than it need be.

She continued down the corridor beside him with no idea of where they were. Still in the hospital, she assumed, although they'd walked along a high, win-dowed bridge from one building to another.

'Were your bags sent up here?'

The question didn't make sense.

'My bags?'

'Suitcase! Belongings! I assume you came with spare clothing and a toothbrush at least.'

Nell stopped walking and looked around vaguely. She had her handbag over her shoulder, having slung it across her chest as she'd run to help, managing to keep hold of it until Yasmeen had put it in a locker while she herself had been in ER.

'I left my suitcase at the airport when the siren sounded. Yasmeen wanted me to wait, but I knew I should help.'

Kal made another exasperated noise.

'You never did have any common sense,' he grumbled, walking on again so she was forced to follow. 'Tucking lame ducks under your wing, taking in strays—you'd give away your shoes if someone needed them.'

'Well, now I have, I suppose,' Nell said, trying to lighten Kal's angry mood, although she was feeling so exhausted she wondered why she bothered. 'That's if the person who picked it up did need them and didn't just take the case for the sake of it.'

Kal made a growly noise under his breath and stopped at a door. He pulled a ring of keys from his pocket and fitted one in the lock.

'This is a master key and I can't give it to you, but if there's no key on the table inside, I'll get someone to bring one to you in the morning.'

In the morning?

'Isn't it already morning?' she asked.

'Tomorrow morning,' Kal said gruffly. 'It's close to midnight, local time. You've worked through a night and day.'

He opened the door on a pleasantly furnished living room with a small kitchen at the far end. 'Bedrooms and bathrooms through there.' He waved his hand towards a door off to the right. 'You'll find toiletries in both bathrooms and bathrobes in the bedroom cupboards.'

'First-class hotel stuff,' Nell said lightly, wondering how soon he'd leave. Tiredness swamped her and she wasn't sure she'd have the energy to shower before she collapsed into bed.

'First class doesn't begin to describe the job you've done for us since you arrived,' he said, and a gruffness in his voice made her turn to look at him. The pain in his eyes hurt her heart and she swayed towards him, wanting more than anything to hold him and ease away that pain.

He caught her shoulders and held her away, still looking at her, his face hardening, the pain shrouded behind his heavy eyelids.

'Unfortunately we'll need more help from you—at least until we can get some other burns experts here—so get some sleep.' He spoke harshly, as if he resented the fact she was needed, and in her exhausted state this attitude confused her.

'I don't mind helping,' she offered.

'Get some sleep,' he repeated, then his hands dropped and he turned and walked away, swinging back to face her as he opened the door.

'If you need anything lift the phone and press one for the apartment block's reception office. They'll send up food now if you want it, or when you wake. Press four for me. My apartment is next door but if I'm not there, the call will be switched to the office, and whoever answers will page me.'

The door closed behind him but, tired as she was, Nell couldn't move. For a long time she stared at the door—at where he'd been—then with a shrug of her shoulders she headed not for the bathroom but for the phone. With a six-hour time difference, it would be early morning in

Australia. She'd stolen time from patients and phoned from downstairs to let the family know she'd arrived safely and to assure them she hadn't been involved in the accident. This time she needed to phone to check on Patrick before she had a shower.

Patrick!

She turned and stared at the door again, while a shiver of presentiment feathered along her spine.

There's a reason she's here and I'm not going to like it.

The words echoed in Kal's head as he made his way back down to the ward to check on the patients one last time before he, too, grabbed some sleep. The other thing he didn't like was the way his mind seemed to be producing a running commentary on the situation, not the accident situation—he was handling that quite well—but the Nell situation.

Why shouldn't it be that she was simply the best person for the Brisbane hospital to send? Or that their relationship had prompted an interest in his country and curiosity had brought her here?

Not for one minute do you believe either of those explanations! the voice in his head said, and a queasy feeling in Kal's stomach told him his instinct agreed.

But this wasn't the time to be looking a gift horse in the mouth—Nell was here and from what he'd seen of her at work today, they couldn't have had a better person helping out.

Yasmeen arrived only minutes after the breakfast Nell had ordered—laden with bags and parcels.

'The chief sent me to the shops,' she said in an awed

voice. 'He said I was to get you clothes. He said good quality and to get you slacks so you wouldn't feel out of place in the hospital, but some loose dresses for you to relax in at home, and some nightclothes and underwear. I bought different sizes and can take back what doesn't fit.'

Nell shook her head as a porter followed Yasmeen into the apartment, with more parcels in his arms and carrier bags dangling from his fingers.

'It's a wonder he didn't bring the whole store to me,' Nell muttered.

'Oh, he was going to,' Yasmeen said, totally serious, although Nell had been joking. 'But I said I didn't think you'd like it. That you'd be embarrassed. So he phoned a place and got it to open early, and I was the only person there.'

'That must have been fun and, yes, I would have been embarrassed,' Nell assured the anxious woman. 'But I can't try on all this stuff now. I've slept for hours longer than I intended. I need to be in the burns unit.'

'You've slept for about six hours,' Yasmeen reminded her. 'Same as me. But I didn't have a long flight from Australia before the accident sent us into chaos.'

'Good thing we're doctors and used to lack of sleep,' Nell said, emptying parcels onto the lounge and fishing through them for clothes that might be suitable. 'It's underwear I need. I can just wear scrubs until my suitcase turns up.'

'It won't turn up,' Yasmeen told her, handing her a bag with underwear in it. 'And if you don't wear the clothes I bought, the chief will blame me.'

'Blackmail?' Nell said, but yesterday's emergency had forged a bond between them and she smiled as she said it, then grabbed a pair of navy slacks and a loose fitting T-shirt, took the bag of underwear and headed for her bedroom.

The female staff she'd seen yesterday had been in navy slacks and tunic tops, and she'd realised that was acceptable dress code for women who when they went out in public would probably wear long robes over their house clothes. She should show respect for their customs by dressing the same way.

'You can't have slept for six hours if you've done all this shopping,' she said, pulling her hair into a tight knot behind her head as she came back into the living room, dressed and ready to go.

'I left the hospital before you,' the other woman said, then she smiled and Nell knew she, too, felt the bond between them, a bond that had bridged the boundaries of nationalities and cultures.

They walked swiftly back across the other bridge—the one between the living quarters and the hospital—Yasmeen leading Nell to the new burns unit, where the state-of-the-art equipment made Nell feel envious.

'The fifteen we have here will all need grafts. I've taken uninjured skin from some of them and the lab is already working on growing it. We've two types of interactive burn dressings we can use in the meantime—the new ones that promote wound healing of the body tissues—but we've been waiting for your advice on which patients to treat with which dressing.'

Kal delivered this information. He was standing right in front of her, a trolley laden with equipment by his side.

'We have a treatment room, a small theatre and bathing facilities here in the unit, and rooms where family members can stay. We're arranging to fly in a family member for all the patients who aren't local so they have emotional support.'

One look at him was enough to tell Nell he hadn't slept, although he was clean-shaven now except for the very short, neatly trimmed beard and moustache around his mouth.

Traditional, she knew, from the time long ago when she'd tried to persuade him to shave it off so she could see how he looked without it!

'You've done well,' she assured him, then, not daring to suggest he needed sleep, she said instead, 'With your permission, I'll take over now. I'll check the status of each patient and prioritise them again for surgery.'

She glanced at the trolley.

'You've pressure bandages as well as the artificial skin, but will there be enough?'

'More of everything is being flown in, and a group of Spanish doctors and nurses should be on the way this afternoon or tomorrow.'

Nell nodded. It was now common practice for specialist doctors from other countries to help in medical emergencies worldwide.

'I'd like to see all the patients,' Nell said, because although she'd suggested it earlier, Kal had not agreed. Now *he* nodded.

'Yasmeen and I will accompany you. I have surgeons standing by if you want to start debriding burnt tissue.'

'It will depend on the patient's status,' Nell reminded him. 'Some will be able to withstand the trauma of surgery but with others we might have to wait. Three to five days post-burn is still acceptable for surgery, although current thinking is to get it done as soon as possible.'

Yasmeen led the way, and they went from bed to bed,

Nell impressed by how efficiently the patients were being nursed, with one staff member to every patient and computerised records up on a screen beside each bed.

'I've removed blisters on this and several other patients,' Kal told her when they stopped by the bed of a teenage girl with severe second-degree burns to her face. 'I know it's a contentious issue, whether the blistered skin aids healing, but my experience suggests the prostaglandin in the blister fluid promotes deeper burns, and on her face—'

He broke off, obviously anxious, and Nell was quick to agree she'd have done the same for the girl. She checked the computer screen.

'The dry dressing is great and I see you're using aspirin for its anti-prostaglandin effect. I'd have gone the same way. What is important is that nurses know to keep cutting back the dressing as the wound heals so the patient isn't tempted to play with a loose edge or pull at it to peel it off. The same goes for the dressings we'll put on grafts, although the dressings on them are harder to get to as we have to immobilise grafted areas.'

While Nell explained this to Kal, Yasmeen was talking to the patient in her own language. As tears welled up in the girl's dark eyes, Nell turned enquiringly to Kal.

'Her parents and brother didn't make it,' he said, his voice hard with frustrated anger. 'We're looking for other relations, but it's difficult with just the plane's manifest to work from. Many people book their seats over the internet these days and although the airline company has contact phone numbers, the number, as in this case, is often of the family home.'

'And no one's there to answer,' Nell said quietly, touching the girl's bandaged hand.

She moved on, knowing there were patients who needed more of her attention. She had to decide which ones might be stable enough to begin the lengthy, painful business of debriding burnt flesh and attaching skin grafts.

'Tell me about the grafts,' Kal said, as they looked at the legs of a woman who had severe burns on the fronts of her legs, particularly around her knees. 'This woman has good skin on her back and buttocks we can use, and we can mesh the skin to make it go further, but we can't use mesh on some places, can we?'

Nell studied the patient, thinking of the instrument called a dermatone that could divide the skin into infinitely thin layers, and how these layers could then be meshed—cut and stretched to go further.

'We never use mesh on the face because it doesn't heal as well.' Nell answered part of the question while examining the woman's arms. 'Generally, we use split-thickness skin grafts on the face or neck or areas where it's in the patient's interests to have a cosmetically good result. Skin from the back or buttocks is good for grafting, but I wonder if in this case we shouldn't take skin from her arm. Could you explain to her I want to push her sleeve up?'

Kal spoke to the woman, taking her hand and looking into her eyes as he introduced Nell and explained.

The woman patted his hand, as if she'd been done the favour, and pushed up the long sleeve of the hospital gown.

'The problem is,' Nell said, running her finger over the woman's smooth, unburnt skin, 'that the graft site—where we take the skin from—is always more painful during recovery than the wound site and just as susceptible to infection. So if we take skin off her back and immobilise her legs to stop the grafts shifting, how's she going to lie?'

Kal shook his head, and smiled ruefully at Nell.

'I knew it was a specialist field, but that's common sense. I should have thought of it.'

'You can't think of everything, but now you know, I think you can start with this woman. She's fit enough in herself to stand an anaesthetic and while you've got her under, you can take off all the burnt tissue, do a small graft from her arm to this area here above the knee. Because the knee needs flexibility, you're better going with a full-thickness graft which has more elasticity. We use epinephrine and thrombin to control the bleeding from the donor site, and xeroform gauze and heat-lamp treatments to help heal the site.'

Kal nodded and spoke to the woman again, then smiled at Nell.

A smile shouldn't make me feel as if the sun's come out, she thought, especially here and now, but before she could pursue this reaction, he was questioning her again.

'Now, if we're taking all the burnt tissue off and only grafting that small area, what's best to use on the rest of the wound?'

'An allograft—false skin—or one of the new preparations that promote wound healing, or maybe, if it's suitable, some of my spray-on skin.'

She smiled at him.

'You didn't think I'd let you go into Theatre without me, did you? I'll be with you and whatever other surgeons you can muster through this first op, though there are other things more important than surgery for me to do after that.'

'Other things more important than surgery!' he grumbled, and this time Nell's reaction was one of remembered pleasure. She and Kal had worked well together all those years ago. It had been their shared dedication to the job that had brought them together—that and an attraction that Nell had never felt before.

Or since, she admitted honestly to herself as Kal spoke again to their patient.

A nurse was sent to get an anaesthetist and a young resident told to prepare the patient for surgery, while Nell moved on, seeing the rest of the patients in the special unit.

'I know it was set up for this reason,' she said to Yasmeen, 'but you could hardly have expected to have to ever deal with this many burn-injured people at once.'

Yasmeen told her about the oil fire and Nell understood that it was for a large-scale emergency Kal had started the unit.

Just in time, as it had turned out...

The patient she thought of as 'her' man was the last she saw. Tucked into a corner of the ward, with mobile equipment monitoring him, Nell almost cheered to see him still alive. But she forgot about cheering when she saw his respiratory function was still poor.

'I'd like to do a fibre-optic bronchoscopy to check his upper respiratory tract, then a proper lung scan. There might be pockets of air trapped in his lungs by obstructions of some kind.'

'I'll arrange it,' Yasmeen told her, giving orders in her own language, though Nell had realised by now that most of the staff spoke some English. 'They must be ready for you in Theatre.'

Nell glanced at her watch but, though she'd set it to local time on the flight, the time didn't seem to mean anything to her. She'd work and then she'd sleep and eventually the days and nights would sort themselves out and her body clock would adjust itself.

But as she was shown into the theatre area by a young nurse, and she saw Kal scrubbing up on the other side of the room, she wondered about his night and day—his body clock.

'You haven't slept—are you up to this?' she demanded, and heard a gasp of what sounded like shock from the theatre sister who was holding out Kal's gown.

Kal turned and grinned at her, the smile lighting up his exhausted face.

'You've shocked Sister Aboud,' he chided. 'Sister Aboud thinks very highly of me and would never speak to me like that.'

Nell smiled at the sister, who was now looking extremely embarrassed.

'When I knew him, he was a fellow student—a postgrad surgical nobody just like me,' she explained, having known from the gasp the woman could understand English.

But the woman didn't seem appeased, and throughout the operation, which was watched by half a dozen other surgeons, she cast doubtful glances Nell's way, as if wondering what the intruder was doing in her theatre.

'Thanks,' Kal said quietly, when they'd done all they could at the moment for the woman. 'You've set me on the right track for future ops.'

'Once the Spanish team gets here, you'll have specialist burns surgeons,' Nell reminded him. 'But in the meantime, that's enough for one day. If you don't get some sleep, you'll collapse on top of a patient and then he or she will sue for injuries sustained in hospital and—'

Kal had pulled off his cap and mask and looked down

at her, and the flow of light banter stopped, the words dried up by the expression in his eyes. They burned into hers, seeming to see past all her defences, deep, deep down into her soul.

'I will go and sleep,' he said quietly, 'when I am satisfied all is well in my hospital.'

Uh-oh! Nell thought as he swept away. Was I just put in my place?

But 'mind your own business' hadn't been the message in his eyes. That message had been personal.

Scorchingly personal!

At least he was gone and she could relax and do her job. She stripped off her theatre gear and headed back to the ward, ready to take up where she'd left off, but when she entered the procedures room, ready to insert a nasogastric tube into a patient, Kal was there.

'You need to sleep,' she told him yet again, cross because, at a time when she needed to be fully focussed on her work, Kal's presence was proving a distraction. Physically, because her skin burned—bad analogy—when he was near, and mentally because parts of her mind kept thinking of why she was there—the why that had nothing to do with the burns unit.

'I'm a surgeon and I'm needed here,' he snapped back. 'Now, let's get to work.'

'Kal, there's nothing the doctors here can't handle at the moment. None of the other severely burned patients are well enough for major surgery. The rest of today's jobs are medical, getting patients stabilised, working out their nutritional needs and starting tube feeding. Even those well enough to take food by mouth probably won't be able to eat enough to take in the calories they need—

we're talking 3000 to 4000 calories a day. I need a dietician up here to work out their caloric intake and the individual formulas for each patient.'

'Working on the weight of the patient and the severity of their burns?' Kal said. 'Do you use the total body surface area affected in the figuring of their requirements?'

'Yes, it's one of the most important factors, because the extent of the injury determines what the body is losing, particularly in protein.'

'And the problems associated with tube feeding?'

Was he testing her? He would know this stuff. She studied him for a moment before answering, but looking directly at him made her heart feel fluttery so she turned back to the patient on the table.

'Aspiration's the most dangerous—the head of the bed needs to be elevated at thirty degrees and gastric residuals measured frequently—then, too, the tube placement needs to be checked.'

She managed a smile.

'It will drive your head of nursing mad but I think these patients are going to need one-on-one nursing for some time to come.'

Why was he testing her? Kal wished she hadn't smiled. And how the blazes was he going to get the staff to provide one-on-one nursing for any length of time?

He couldn't think straight. He *must* be tired, but he wasn't going to have Nell erupting back into his life and telling him what to do. Though he knew he'd be better off getting some sleep now, and working when she was sleeping. That way he didn't have to go through an experience like the one he'd had in Theatre, where working next to her had been so distracting he'd wanted to swear long and hard.

Which really would have shocked Sister Aboud!

'I'll make sure we have the nurses,' he said, dragging his mind back to the issue at hand. 'There are two small private hospitals, mainly used by expats, and both have offered to lend us staff.'

Nell smiled again, but he knew it was with the pleasure of knowing that the staff would be provided. Then the smile warmed as she ordered gently, 'Go, Khalil. Go and sleep. By tomorrow we'll have more patients well enough to begin excision and grafting, and once that starts it's an ongoing process as we can only do small areas of burn every two to three days.'

No one had ever said his name as Nell said it. Perhaps she was going through a mid-life crisis and was revisiting a lost love.

Reviving a lost love?

Renewing a lost love?

Excitement soared as the falcon had soared, then dropped like a stone as he told himself not to be fanciful. Even if Nell was no longer married, she'd always known of his commitment to family and she'd certainly assume *he* was. Hadn't he told her that's how things worked in his country? One married for life. Sometimes more than once, that was allowable, but marriage was for ever.

Most of the time!

Nell worked through the day and into the night, with Yasmeen and with doctors she didn't know, trying to keep patients alive being the first priority, stabilising them so they'd be well enough for surgery the second. At some stage Kal came back and ordered her to leave the ward, but when she returned the following morning and saw him there, dishevelled and unshaven, she knew he'd stayed on in her place.

'Get some sleep,' she said to him, realising from the way other staff treated him that no one else would dare tell him what to do, although she seemed to be making a habit of it. 'You won't be any use in the state you're in, and there are other surgeons willing to work on any patient well enough for surgery. Skin grafting takes a clear head and a steady hand, Kal, and you've got neither at the moment.'

For a moment she thought he was going to argue, but then he turned and walked away.

'You know him from before?' Yasmeen asked, having watched this small interchange with wonderment.

'We met while he was studying in Australia. Out there he was just a fellow student, not the Grand Poo Bah or whatever he is here.'

'He's not a Poo Bah, or whatever you said, but a sheik,' Yasmeen protested, and Nell regretted her attempted levity. Yasmeen had already demonstrated that she held Kal in some kind of awe. 'His family, they've been our rulers for generations. It is unusual he became a doctor, but he's a good doctor and he's made the hospital what it is, insisting on the best of everything.'

'He's certainly got that,' Nell agreed, but uneasiness stirred within her. She'd always known Kal's family had some kind of standing in this country, although he'd never boasted about them in any way. It was something she'd guessed from his bearing and sometimes from his attitude.

But the ruling family?

Oh, hell! Would that complicate things?

She didn't need, or even particularly want, them to acknowledge Patrick, but she might one day want some of their bone marrow...

Damn!

'Dr Warren, could you come?'

A young nurse drew her towards a patient with twenty per cent burns to his body.

'Here!' The nurse pointed, showing her a small area of redness near the patient's thigh, the first sign of an infection.

Thanking the woman, Nell turned her attention to the task of fighting this invader before it took over the man's body. All thoughts of Kal and his family were forgotten...

CHAPTER THREE

IT WAS late afternoon, and she was unlocking her apartment when Kal emerged from his, refreshed from the sleep but more confused than ever about Nell.

'Do you keep an apartment here because the hospital demands so much of your time?' she asked. 'Wouldn't you have been better going home and having a proper break?'

'This is my home,' he said, looking into the eyes of the woman he'd thought he'd never see again, seeing the dark rims around the irises of her clear grey eyes and tiredness in the bloodshot whites. But the question wouldn't wait any longer.

'Why are you here, Nell?'

She hesitated, just long enough for him to suspect she was going to fob him off.

'I don't want some tale about spray-on skin!' he growled. 'I want the truth.'

The pale eyes pleaded with him.

'I want to tell you, Kal,' she whispered, what little colour there was in her face draining from it. 'But now?'

'Now!' he said, listening to the voice in his head suggesting again that this woman was up to something, and ignoring common sense which reminded him that the hospital desperately needed her expertise.

But she was antagonising him just by being here—making him want to touch her, to take her in his arms and hold her, remembering her body, kiss her, remembering her lips...

'I need a coffee,' she said, walking into her apartment but not shutting the door in his face.

He followed her, and saw the bags and parcels strewn across the couch. He should at least let her unpack. And when was she going to eat?

After she's told me what's going on—that's when!
'Coffee?'

No smile accompanied the offer but that was just as well.
'Please.'

He didn't smile either, but he watched her move as she filled the kettle, her litheness and economy of movement unchanged by the years they'd spent apart. He noticed her hands as she spooned instant coffee into mugs. No rings, but she'd just come from the ward and few staff wore rings at work as they could tear the fragile rubber gloves.

She concentrated on the simple task, not looking at him, not even glancing up to ask him how he liked it.

She pushed a cup towards him, then put sugar on the table.

'There doesn't appear to be any milk anywhere, but I don't mind drinking it black.'

He heard her speak but the anguish in her eyes suggested they weren't the words she wanted to say, so he waited, sipping at his coffee. The old Nell would weigh things up, practise what she wanted to say, but usually, in the end, it would all come out in a rush, as if she was afraid if she stopped to sort the words into the practised order, she'd lose them.

Her parting speech to him had been testimony to that. 'I'll love you for ever—that's all I can say.'

The words had burst from a throat constricted with tears, but the letter she'd pressed into his hands—a letter he'd read and reread on the trip home until it had fallen to pieces in his hands—had contained the rehearsed speech, with words like 'always knew it couldn't be for ever between us' and 'totally understand' and 'admire your loyalty and devotion to your family and your commitment to your promise'.

He watched her struggle for a moment, then it came, a statement so abrupt he had trouble processing it.

'We have a son.'

There was a deafening silence before he could answer.

'We have a son?'

He knew the loudly spoken echo had been his—it was his voice—but the sentence still made no sense.

'A boy. I was pregnant when you left. I didn't know at the time and when I did find out I couldn't tell you because you were going home to get married—you were probably already married by then. It was part of the bargain with your parents, and I couldn't ruin that for you or have you torn between two loyalties or spoil your marriage with that kind of news, and I thought you'd never need to know—'

Kal halted the flow of words the only way he could, by grabbing her shoulders and giving her a little shake.

'Stop right there!' he ordered. 'Right now!'

His voice was rising with his anger. No, his anger was rising much faster, hot and dangerous as the flow of new lava spewing from a volcano.

'I have a *son*? You were pregnant and you didn't tell me? By what right did you make that decision? You, who knew my feelings about family! About blood ties! *My* son, and you kept him from me? How could you? How dared you?'

Nell felt the heat of his rage burning through her T-shirt, as fierce as the flames she'd watched on her arrival. She stared into the furious face of the father of her son and imagined she could see a thousand generations of Bedouin warriors ranging behind him in defence of the family honour.

'Kal—' she began, anxious to explain—aware she'd made a hash of it. But he thrust her away, so roughly she had to catch the bench to stop from falling.

'Kal!' His name was a plaintive plea on her trembling lips, but he'd moved away, striding towards the door, though when he'd flung it open he turned back to glare at her, anger still reverberating in his deep voice as he spoke.

'And where is he now, my son? If he's stuck in some boarding school…'

An unspoken threat hovered in the air, but Nell ignored it, desperate to calm things down so she could get to the really important part of this revelation.

'He's with my parents. We've always lived with them so they could be there for him while I worked.'

'Which was, of course, important for your fulfillment, no doubt, and your self-esteem and all the other palaver you so-called liberated women go on about.'

That was too much altogether for Nell. Forget calming him down.

'I'd say at least half of the doctors I've met in your hospital are women, so don't make this a women's lib issue, Kal! I've worked to support my son, and to provide him with a good life.'

'And I couldn't have done that?' Smooth as silk, his voice now—smooth and somehow scary. 'Couldn't have given him far more than your puny salary would ever have provided for him? And what's his name, this son of mine? Warren, after some man you married to gratify your own desires?'

'Get out of here!' Nell ordered, clinging desperately to the last vestiges of control. 'Now!'

She should go after him—try to explain—but she was so exhausted, both from work and the debilitating effect of the fierce confrontation, that Nell sank down onto the lounge amidst the parcels Yasmeen had brought, and buried her face in her hands.

The worst thing about it was he was right. She *had* known how he felt about family. She *had* known that if she'd told him, he'd have returned in an instant and insisted on marrying her.

But what would that have meant to his family? Just how badly would they have taken it, and what damage would it have done to Kal's position within it, when family meant so much to him? Family and honour! Honour was a word not often used in her life but to Kal it was the backbone of his existence. And Nell had known that Kal not marrying the woman to whom he had been betrothed would have brought dishonour both on the woman and on his family…

She heard the sound of a key in the door and raised her head.

He was back.

'And your parents? Are they still in the same place?'

Nell struggled to her feet.

'Why? What are you going to do?'

'I'm sending someone to get my son.'

Fear for Patrick propelled Nell across the room. She grasped Kal's arm.

'You'd kidnap him?'

He shook off her hands

'Don't be so melodramatic. I'll merely send a plane and some of my people to take care of him on the journey. You'll phone your family to let them know what's happening.'

Nell couldn't believe she was hearing this.

'You can't do that. You can't just fly into a country and take a child out of it.'

'If he's my son, he's hardly a child.'

Nell gasped at the implication of his words, but she didn't have time to protest. She had too much to explain.

'Kal, we need to sit down and talk rationally about this. There's so much you don't know—so much to explain—but I can't talk to you when you're in this mood.'

'Then don't talk to me. The time to talk was fourteen years ago, Nell. You've left it too late.'

He saw the pain of his words etching lines down her cheeks, deep as acid burns, but the rage within him was too hot and strong to prevent him hurting her.

'Kal?'

She touched his arm again and for a moment, hearing his name on her lips, feeling her fingers on his arm, he almost weakened, then he remembered this woman had denied him his son for thirteen years.

He could *never* weaken.

He walked away instead—out of her apartment. She hadn't answered his question but the hospital would have records of Nell's address, and the boy would be there. The plane was always on standby. One phone call and it would be ready to roll by the time his staff reached the airport. The new jet would make good time, and with the time difference they'd arrive late afternoon in Australia. The Spanish burns team was due to start work at the hospital in the morning so he'd have time to go to the airport and meet the boy.

He'd take Nell—there'd be awkwardness and he'd need her to smooth things over on this first meeting...

He lifted the phone to call the airport then heard the knock on the door. He knew it was Nell and hesitated, then put down the receiver and crossed the room.

Nell looked around. The apartment looked very similar to the one she was using, except that books were stacked on the low coffee-table and on the end tables beside the couch. Stacked, too, on the kitchen divider—the books the only sign someone used the place.

She looked at Kal, wanting to ask why he needed so many books in what had to be a place he used only occasionally, but what Kal did or didn't need in his apartment wasn't her concern.

And he'd always had books—always been reading—not only about medicine, but about anything and everything.

It was a trait Patrick had inherited...

Thinking of Patrick steeled her for the confrontation. She studied Kal's face desperately seeking some kind of softening, but it remained implacably set against her, granite hard, while his eyes still burned with anger.

She took a deep breath and rushed the words towards him.

'Patrick has cancer. He's in remission right now, but he needs constant monitoring.'

Just saying it brought back the nightmare of the last eighteen months—the initial diagnosis, then the treatment, the joy of the first remission so soon after treatment and then the devastation of the relapse. She could feel her heart beating erratically and a hard lump growing in her throat, but if she showed weakness for one second, Kal would pounce.

He watched her swallow and wondered what it had cost her to say those words. Pain was squeezing *his* rib cage and he didn't know the boy.

'He has cancer and even then you didn't think to contact me?' he asked, the pain confusing him because it seemed to be dampening his anger, and he needed his anger to handle this situation. 'What kind of cancer?'

'Leukaemia. T-cell ALL. He's in remission at the moment, but it's the second remission and if it fails he'll need—'

And suddenly it all became clear.

'A bone-marrow transplant! You keep a son from me for thirteen years and now you're here to beg me to help him?'

He flung the accusation at her then frowned.

'But parents are no good—you need a sibling for a match.'

His eyes narrowed.

'Are you telling me you want another child? A child of mine? You've come here for, what, a month, hoping to get me to father another child which you'll then take away from me. And is this fair to this child—?'

Nell stopped him, which was probably just as well. His head was all over the place and he had no idea how he felt about any of this.

'It's not about another child, Kal. I didn't even think of that. Anyway, there's only a thirty to thirty-five per cent chance of a sibling being a perfect match. But the procedures are much better for mismatched bone-marrow transplants these days. Parents usually have a three out of six HLA match—the human leukocyte antigens that are the genetic markers on the white blood cells—and that's really not enough. Not yet, although if we can't do better, the specialists are willing to go with a parent's bone marrow. The problem is, although he's on a register for donors, he has some HLA antigens in his blood that aren't found in Australia. Apparently…'

She stopped, as if she found the rest of the bizarre explanation impossible to continue. Well, he wasn't going to help her, not one little bit. The more she talked, the more his gut twisted at the thought of this son he didn't know suffering so much. T-cell ALL—acute lymphoblastic leukaemia with involvement of the T-cells. His mind was recalling all he knew of it, considering the damage it did, and the worse damage the treatment could cause.

'Apparently these antigens are found more frequently in a specific ethnic group and though he might not need bone marrow—this remission might last, he might be cured—I couldn't take the risk, Kal. I had to find out if you had a bone-marrow donor programme over here, and if maybe someone on it… Maybe you or someone in your family even…'

Kal stared at her, seeing the strain in her pale exhausted face, hating her yet wanting to hold and comfort her.

Dangerous thoughts, dismissed immediately.

'Don't expect me to feel sorry for you,' he snapped. 'There was no need at all for you to have gone through this on your own. And where's Mr Warren? Where does he fit in? If you are married, why are you still living with your parents?'

He stepped towards her because anger had returned a thousandfold, though this time it was a different kind of anger—jealous anger—so unexpected it drove him beyond all bounds of decency and common sense.

'Have you left him, too? And why's that, Nell? Did he not kiss you like this?'

He seized her by the shoulders and dragged her towards his body, bending his head and capturing her lips in a hard, possessive kiss.

Tasting Nell again! He didn't drink but could there be more intoxication in alcohol than there was in kissing Nell?

Her lips parted, perhaps in protest, but he refused to release her, feeling her body soften, then slump against him, feeling her lips respond and a faint puff of air as she murmured his name.

One hand moved from her shoulders, his finger trailing downwards to the soft mound of a breast, teasing at the nipple through the clothing she wore, his mind gloating as he heard her sudden intake of breath.

'Did he not make you whimper when he touched you, Nell? Is that it?'

She broke away so suddenly it shocked him back to some measure of sanity, but regret at his behaviour was all mixed up with regret that the kiss had ended. Until he saw her face—saw disappointment etched into it and deep shadows of sadness in her lovely eyes.

'Nell!'

She turned away from him and walked towards the door, and though he followed and caught up, he didn't dare touch her to stop her leaving, for fear he'd need to hold her close again.

'Let me know if you think you can help.'

She threw the words over her shoulder, but he heard the thickness of tears in them and his heart ached for her—yearned to comfort her—but how?

'Nell?'

She turned now and he saw the tears, not streaming down her cheeks—oh, no, she was far too strong for that. But they were pooled in her eyes, valiantly held back, and fear joined anger in his heart.

Had his rash words and harsh behaviour ruined any chance they might have had of being friends again?

You don't want her for a friend but for a lover!

This idea spun him even further out of his orbit, and Nell was standing there, looking at him. Waiting for what he had to say?

For an apology?

She's the one who should be apologising.

'We have a fledgling donor programme but I can look into expanding it. And of course I'll have the test,' he said, aware how lame the words sounded, and knowing it wasn't what he wanted to say.

Or not all of it.

Nell nodded, then turned away, continuing on to her apartment. She knew her back was straight but inside she felt as if her bones were crumbling and all the soft parts of her melting.

With anger *and* desire.

How dared Kal kiss her like that? That was the anger talking.

But why had she been so stupid as to pull away? That

was desire. A desire so fierce and strong, so easily rekindled even after fourteen years, that she *had* very nearly whimpered in his arms. How *could* she have been so weak? This wasn't about her, and physical gratification. This was about Patrick.

'But there'll be some conditions!'

She was halfway through the door when she heard this rider, and she spun around, aware he was close—probably too close—but needing to see his face, to see if he could possibly mean he'd attach provisos to an act that could save his son's life.

His eyes, their colour still a fascination to her—pale brown like good brandy—challenged her to defy his statement, challenged her to ask what kind of conditions. But she'd had enough of Kal and the emotion-entangling games he was playing.

'Whatever!' she said, and shrugged carelessly, although her heart was breaking. This man wasn't the Kal she'd loved and whose memory had shone so brightly in her life for the last fourteen years, but there was no way she'd let him witness her distress.

'Marriage!' he growled as she turned away once again. 'We'll legitimise my son!'

This time she couldn't face him. Here was an offer she'd fantasised about so often over the years, although now it felt repugnant.

'As your second wife?' she snapped, angry because with that one word he'd killed the dreams she'd had. 'Or would it be third? Or fourth, perhaps? Changed your mind about monogamy since your idealistic youth?'

She continued walking into the apartment as she spoke, but heard his footsteps on the carpet behind her so when he put his hand—just one hand this time—on her shoulder and spun her around, she wasn't as startled by his touch as she'd been earlier.

'My only wife,' he snapped right back at her. 'My other wife and I divorced. Our marriage never worked out. All I did was make her unhappy—too unhappy even to conceive a child. I blamed myself—I blamed that destructive, intangible, idiotic concept you westerners call love—for the whole debacle. Remember love, Nell?'

'Yes, I do remember love!' she retorted. 'And it's not some destructive, intangible or idiotic concept, but emotion, Kal. Real emotion! Remember emotion?'

'Emotion?' he queried, stepping closer. Dangerously close. 'Emotion, Nell, or sex?'

And once again he put both hands on her shoulders, only this time he didn't drag her closer, but stepped to narrow the gap between them, so that their bodies were all but touching, so close Nell could feel the desire between them, like static electricity arcing in dry air.

She knew he was going to kiss her again even before she saw his head bend towards her, and although his hands were non-restraining on her shoulders, she couldn't move.

If he kisses you again you're gone, her head yelled at her, but her body burned for a touch it should have forgotten long ago, and her breasts ached for his hands to hold them.

He kissed her again.

This time he'd seduce her, Kal decided. He gentled his lips so they tempted and teased, the harsh demands of the earlier kiss hidden behind this provocative flirtation. He drew her closer, feeling her body melt against his, fitting his contours as if they'd been designed as one then split apart into male and female.

Her lips seemed to swell in lushness, her tongue touched his, timidly at first, then teasing and enticing. He knew his arousal would be hard against her belly—knew she'd be aware he wanted her—his desire matched in intensity by hers, if the small gasping noises she was making were any indication.

Then she whispered his name and whatever restraint he might have been clinging to gave way altogether. He swept her into his arms and carried her through to the bedroom, tossing her on the bed, then pulling off her shoes and throwing them aside, running his hands up her legs until he came to the waistband of her slacks, unfastening, unzipping, reefing the long trousers off her.

'Kal!'

If it was a protest it was a half-hearted one, not strong enough to stop his calm, deliberate task of undressing her.

'It is our custom for the bride to be in layers of clothing—a wedding gown, a cap and breastplate of gold, then black robes, covering all her clothes, and veils covering her face. We unwrap our brides as we do a very special parcel.'

The words penetrated the fog of desire that had wrapped around Nell like the veils he spoke of.

'But I am not your bride!' she answered. 'And neither—'

He stopped the words with another kiss, stealing her breath and making a lie of her attempts to stop this unbelievable seduction.

But now that she was sitting, it was easier for him to peel off her T-shirt. Still kissing her to stifle further protests, he unfastened her bra, releasing her breasts. Nell knew she could stop him with a couple of well-chosen words. Although maybe she couldn't! She would have been able to stop the old Kal but this man, intent now on undressing himself, coldly preparing to make love to her—this was a man she didn't know.

So why not stop him?

Shame forced her to admit it was because she wanted him. She wanted to lose herself in him—to forget the last few years with the strain of Patrick's illness, and to escape, if only momentarily, the horror of the fire and the pain and mutilation of the patients she must tend.

Kal was naked, his body hard and lean. He sat beside her on the bed then turned, his eyes unreadable, his lips set in a thin line.

'Are you ready?'

It was such a bizarre question she couldn't answer it. She frowned up at him, but then he put his hand flat on her stomach and her heart lurched at the touch. His hand moved lower, his fingers tangling in her pubic hair, seeking out the aching centre of her womanhood, while his head bent so his tongue could tease her breast.

His fingers explored, his lips nuzzled and sensation transported Nell to a place where thought was impossible, her body a quivering mass of nerve endings, responding to Kal's as if hard-wired to it all those years ago. Electricity tingled in her toes, and her head buzzed with sensation as he drew her with unrelenting mastery to a gasping, shattering climax. Then he entered her, driving deep into the hot, hungry centre of her being, again and again until the waves of orgasm broke once more, swamping her so she had to cling to him, whispering his name into the smooth skin of his shoulder, feeling his own tension build to a final release.

His body relaxed and she wanted to hold him, to feel

his weight on top of her, to keep the closeness for ever, but he rolled away, once again sitting up on the side of the bed, his back towards her.

'There'll be papers to sign, of course, to formalise things, but we're married, you understand.'

It was a statement, not a question, and so coldly uttered Nell shivered, then gathered her scattered wits and sat up herself.

'Married! Don't be ridiculous, Kal. We had sex, nothing more. Two people hungry for each other. Seeking satisfaction and release. Marriage? The very idea of it is ridiculous.'

He turned towards her, his face all hard planes and angles, no sign of post-coital softness despite the shuddering climaxes they'd shared.

'Why did you marry this Warren man if not for sex? Did you love him? Did he leave you? I'm assuming you're not still married to him. You couldn't have changed so much you'd cheat on your husband, and you could have stopped me at any time during that little performance.'

That little performance? Was that all it had been? A performance to show how easily he could dominate her? Of how easily he could manipulate her feelings?

Well, two could play that game! She could be just as cool and detached as he could. It didn't matter that her insides were aglow with satisfaction and her body all but twitching with the hope that it could happen again.

Soon!

'Garth Warren was a good man—a close friend. We'd known each other for a long time, and I thought maybe it would be good for Patrick to have a male influence in his life.'

'I'm glad you didn't use the word father!' Kal growled. 'So what happened to this paragon?'

'Garth? We parted within six months. It wasn't fair to have married him in the first place because I didn't love him, and as things went on I knew I never could. He's remarried to a lovely woman and I'm godmother to their twins.'

'How civilised you westerners are!' The derisive retort was so unlike Kal, Nell wondered if she'd ever really known him. 'Love or no love, if you were my wife, I'd have chained you in a cellar before I let you go.'

'But you did let me go,' Nell reminded him softly.

'You were not my wife, though you would have been if you'd told me of my son.'

He stopped abruptly and turned to her again, his face now puzzled.

'My son. His name is Patrick?'

Nell nodded, wondering if this, too, would make him angry, but all he said was, 'Why?'

'I remembered you telling me of the tutor you'd had, and how it had been his influence that had made you decide to study medicine.' Nell shrugged. 'He seemed to mean a lot to you…'

Kal stood up and left the room. He was forty years old, yet his emotions were as tumultuous as the most raw adolescent's. This woman had thrown his life into total chaos.

First she'd fired his body to such an extent he'd behaved like the barbarian she probably believed him to be. Then she'd fired this rocket into the congealed mess that had once been his mind.

She'd called his son Patrick! Named him after the man who'd given Kal so much. His love of books—the inspiration to do medicine—the strength to break from family tradition by studying something apart from business—and the confidence to bargain with his father to make it possible.

His son was called Patrick.

He left the apartment, aware in the part of him that had always been true to the manners and decency and moral behaviour instilled in him that he had behaved very badly towards Nell. So what if the sex had been unbelievable?

He groaned to himself as he entered his apartment, and, pleased to be diverted from his thoughts, picked up the phone to retrieve the messages signalled by the red flashing light.

The Spanish team was definitely due to arrive the following morning. One of the burn victims in the ICU had died. Two of the less critical patients in other wards were being repatriated to their home countries and Lalla had organised nursing staff to travel with them. His mother would like him to phone her when he had time, and a Mrs Roberts had phoned from Australia.

Mrs Roberts? Nell's mother?

Patrick! Something was wrong with the boy and Mrs Roberts didn't want to tell Nell directly.

He dialled the number that had been left, not thinking for a minute of the time difference, though when a cheerful voice answered the phone he realised it would be morning in Australia.

'Oh, Kal, I am so sorry to bother you, but I've been trying to phone Nell and can't seem to make the receptionist at the hospital understand me. In the end I thought of you. Could you, please, ask her to phone me?'

'Is it Patrick? Is he ill again? Should we come?'

There was an audible gasp, then Mrs Roberts said, 'Oh, she's told you already. I'm so glad. And so sorry, too,

Kal, for the way things turned out. You, her, Patrick—but no, he's fine. He's staying over at a friend's place for a couple of days—they're studying together for a chemistry exam. But Don, Mr Roberts, he's been on a waiting list for a kidney for a long time and they phoned last night to say there was one available. I wanted to let Nell know and to tell her I'd be in touch as soon as the op was done, and also that I've arranged for someone to look after Patrick because I'll want to stay at the hospital as much as possible. My sister, Mary, is arriving this afternoon.'

Maybe it was the distance between them, but Mrs Roberts sounded remarkably calm for a woman whose husband was about to undergo major surgery and whose grandson was in remission from leukaemia.

'Has Mr Roberts been seriously ill? Shouldn't Nell be there? Won't you want her support?'

'I'd like nothing better,' Mrs Roberts said, 'but you don't know Nell too well if you think she'd leave her patients to come home and hold my hand. She knows her dad has the best doctors available, and she knows how much he wanted this—to get off the dialysis—so she'll be worried but she'll be pleased as well. But I don't want her to worry about Patrick.'

'I'll look after Nell, and Patrick, too,' Kal heard himself say. 'She probably hasn't had time to tell you, but I'm thinking of bringing him over here. It seems like a good idea to get to know him while Nell's working in the country.'

Kal knew this was toying with the truth, but found himself driven by something beyond rational thought or reasoning.

'Oh, Kal, that's wonderful. I've been so worried about him—about how he'll handle seeing his grandfather when he comes home from hospital. Patrick has always thought that his grandfather is ten feet tall and bullet-proof. He understands about the operation, of course, and knows Don will need time to recover, but to see him weak—I've been worried about the effect that would have on Patrick.'

Mrs Roberts hesitated and though anger was racing through Kal once again—it should be *he* Patrick looked up to—he knew he had to sound calm and in control.

'Then it will be good all round if he's here,' he said, and was congratulating himself on his composure when Mrs Roberts raised another doubt.

'But what about his tests? Patrick's blood tests and regular check-ups? His medication?'

'Mrs Roberts, I'm a doctor, I live at the hospital, we have some of the best pathologists and oncologists in the world here. You can be very sure that Patrick will be well cared for. Now, let's get the main things sorted out. When is Mr Roberts being admitted and where?'

'We're leaving in ten minutes for All Saints Private. Nell knows the number, but tell her not to keep phoning. I'll be sure to contact her whenever there's any news.'

Kal assured her once again that he'd look after Nell, then offered his private number and his mobile number.

'If I can't take the call, it will switch to a paged message so call me any time—day or night—and leave a number where I can call you back.'

Mrs Roberts said goodbye, and Kal hung up and stared out the window at the bright lights of the city, and beyond them the blackness that was the desert.

He'd done it! He'd made a commitment to see his son.

Not in a particularly honourable way!

Anyway, honourable or not, it was for the best, though, of course, Nell might not agree.

Nell. Over here, helping his people, working at his hospital, while at home her father was about to undergo major surgery. He felt the first stirrings of guilt. His conscience reminded him of his recent behaviour towards her. He even felt a pang of anxiety for her—a wish that he could spare her the pain and worry he knew this news would cause.

Would she be sleeping now?

If so, should he let her sleep? Tell her in the morning, by which time her father's operation might be successfully completed?

Wouldn't that be better than having her lying awake all night, worried and anxious, as she waited for her mother's call?

Though her mother would call him first, not Nell. For some reason he hadn't given Mrs Roberts Nell's direct number. Was it so he could shield Nell if the news was bad? Tell her himself rather than have her hear it over a telephone?

Maybe some of the gentleness Kal had always believed made a man a better person remained, though he'd shown precious little gentleness to Nell earlier.

Still debating whether to tell Nell or not, he walked out of his apartment, his bunch of keys dangling from his fingers. He knocked quietly on her door, a strange thought rising unbidden in his mind.

If she's awake and I tell her and she's upset, then the obvious thing to do would be to stay with her to comfort her through the long anxious hours. He could lie with her, hold her…

He refused to listen to whatever else might be suggested, but quietly unlocked the door, aware of his invasion of Nell's space but needing to see her.

She was sleeping soundly, a sheet across her naked body, her shoulder-length dark hair splayed across the pillow, her lashes black on cheeks so pale he again felt a pang of guilt about what had transpired earlier.

He wouldn't wake her, but he'd sleep close by, his phone set to vibrate rather than ring, so when the news came—and, please, God it would be good—he could tell her straight away.

That decision made, he should move. He knew he should. But the sight of the sleeping woman held him in thrall, and he stood and watched her breathe and thought of all he didn't know about her—and of all the time they'd wasted.

Surprised by what seemed like regret, he searched around inside himself.

No, the anger hadn't gone, and why should it? She'd been wrong not to tell him she was pregnant, but right now her family was in trouble and she was far from home. He backed away into the living room, where he swept all the shopping bags off the lounge and tried it for size. Pulling one of the cushions down for a pillow, he settled on the floor. He slept better in the desert with just the sand beneath him. Sleeping on the floor was no hardship.

It wasn't exactly a snore, more just heavy breathing, loud enough for Nell, when she stirred in her sleep, to notice it.

The sound wasn't close enough to bother her, but she slipped out of bed and was about to go and investigate when she became aware of her naked state. She really should have gone through the clothes Yasmeen had left—the ones in the living room, where the noise was.

She pulled off the top sheet to wrap around her body and tiptoed out. Moonlight lit the room, as it had her bedroom, but in its glow she could see nothing to explain the noise.

Maybe it was just the water pipes…

No, that was definitely a snore. Not a loud snore, more a kind of snort, but definitely a noise made in sleep.

She crept towards the couch, thinking maybe a very small person might be curled up on it, then she saw the figure on the floor.

Kal?

Why had he returned to her apartment?

And what was he doing, sleeping on the floor?

She couldn't think of a logical explanation to either of the questions, but felt contrarily glad that he was here. Oh, he'd spoken harshly—acted harshly too—but she couldn't believe the gentle man who'd lived inside the arrogant one she'd first met in Australia could have disappeared altogether.

She stared at him, bemused by the very different sides of Kal. It had been the arrogant man who'd made the loud noises about marriage.

But the gentle man *was* still there inside him. She'd seen him in action on the ward. Maybe it was only in personal relations that the arrogant man held sway.

She made her way quietly back to bed. She was too tired to consider what Kal might or might not be doing on her floor, or to work out how much or little he'd changed since she'd known him before.

It had been fourteen years after all. Didn't everyone change with time?

Not Kal! her heart prayed, but her body burned with memories of their love-making and she was forced to admit that, yes, he'd changed. The old Kal had been a wild, exciting lover, demanding, yes, but always—well, lover-like. Tender in his whispered words, warmly loving and affectionate in the afterglow of love. Tonight's Kal had been ruthlessly competent, bringing her an almost unendurable pleasure but remote from her—detached— so unemotional she'd felt his coldness sweep across her when he'd drawn away.

So why on earth was he sleeping on her floor?

Penance?

Kal?

Hardly!

Nell went back to bed. Against all common sense she was strangely comforted by the sound of his breathing and she slid quickly into a dreamless sleep.

Less comforting was his news next morning. He was in the kitchen when she came out—again wrapped in the sheet as she needed clean clothes from the parcels in the living room. Beyond him, through the windows, she could see the city, and as she grew closer she could see the parkland surrounding the hospital, gardeners way down below working on keeping it neat and trim.

Why was she thinking about parkland?

So she didn't have to think about Kal being in her apartment?

Or about her reaction to his presence?

'Nell.' His voice was gentle as he stepped towards her, and her heart leapt. He was going to apologise for last night. They could start again. Try to bridge the gulf between them. 'Your mother phoned last night.'

He was close enough to grab her as she whispered, 'Patrick?' Close enough to pull her to him and hold her as he explained.

'Not Patrick, but your father. It's all right. He's OK. Your mother phoned to say they'd found a donor kidney for him and he was going straight in to have the operation. I didn't wake you because she said she'd ring again as soon as it was over. I've just spoken to her—it went well, and he's conscious.'

Nell pulled away and looked up at the man who'd given her this startling news.

'Is that why you slept on the floor?'

Kal nodded, not able to explain the need to be near her.

'Thank you,' Nell said, so formally he knew he'd somehow made things worse, not better, between them. 'I'll phone home now—or phone the hospital. And I'll have to ring Patrick, too. He'll have been worried sick.'

'He's at a friend's place and didn't know until your mother rang to tell him it was successful. Someone called Mary is going to stay at the house with him so your mother can be at the hospital.'

Until I get there, Kal should have added, but he knew Nell would fight him on this. If she'd wanted Patrick to meet his father, she'd have brought him with her on this trip.

He told Nell the name of the hospital he'd written down and waited, but she turned away from him, heading straight for the phone. He could see her fingers trembling as she dialled the numbers, but he couldn't find anything to say to comfort her.

You set the parameters of this relationship with your behaviour last night, the voice in his head reminded him, and he swore under his breath and left the room.

CHAPTER FOUR

ONCE satisfied all was well at home, and buoyed by news that the surgeons were delighted with her father's progress, Nell ordered breakfast, then showered and dressed for work while she waited for it to be delivered.

Concern about her father's continued recovery was keeping other thoughts at bay, and for that she was grateful. But when she entered the burns unit a little later, the first person she saw was Kal, and her body surged with remembered passion, while her heart fluttered with what couldn't possibly be love. How could she still feel love for Kal after his behaviour last night?

You responded last night!

The accusation, silent though it was, reminded her, and remembering made her blush.

'Where will we start?' she said to Yasmeen, anxious to get her mind focussed totally on work. In the past—when Kal had left—she'd used work to blot out her emotions. Now, older and stronger, surely she could do the same.

'With the patients who need surgery?' Yasmeen suggested, and Nell followed her to the bed of the first of these, an airport worker who'd been one of the first onto the burning plane and who, in trying to rescue people, had been badly burned himself.

He had enough unburned skin to take some both for growing new and for grafting. Again, the good skin could be sliced into very fine layers to make it go further.

'The worst burns are on his arms.' Kal had been at the patient's bedside and now he moved a little away to point this out to her.

'Which means if we excise the injured tissue right down to the fascia, taking off the underlying fat, we'll get good blood supply to the graft so a better chance of it taking, but he'll be left with bad disfigurement as the fat layers never grow back and his arms will look so thin they'll be stick-like.'

She looked at Kal.

'Will that matter to him, do you think?'

'He's a young man and good-looking. I think it might,' Yasmeen said, her voice tentative, giving Nell the impression she was shy in Kal's presence—or unused to working closely with him.

'Yasmeen's right,' Kal said, smiling gently at the other doctor, as if he, too, had sensed her diffidence. 'We are a proud people, and perhaps too conscious of our looks. Do you think the risk of performing a shallower, tangential excision and grafting onto the superficial fat is too big to take?'

Nell thought about it for a moment, her gaze straying back to the patient in the bed. He *was* a good-looking young man.

'OK, here are the facts. We'll get more blood loss with the tangential, so we have to be sure he's strong enough to cope with that. We also need to have extra blood on standby in Theatre. And if the graft doesn't take, we'll have to try again, and each time we lose a graft and have to try another one, the wound gets bigger. But I'm happy for you to go that way if you both believe it's in his best interests long term.'

Kal nodded then looked at Yasmeen again.

'Let's ask him,' Yasmeen suggested, and she turned to the very ill young man lying in the bed. She spoke briskly in the fluid-sounding language, and though Nell had found a tutor to teach Patrick Arabic from the time he'd been a young child, she understood very few of the words herself.

'Least scarring,' Yasmeen confirmed. 'I'll stay here and do the paperwork to get him to Theatre. The patient in bed six is the one you should see next.'

'You're sure you're all right to be working?' Kal asked as he accompanied Nell to the next patient.

'Better working than brooding,' Nell assured him. 'At least here my mind is fully occupied with patients and I don't have time to worry about Dad.'

'Fully occupied, Nell?' he murmured, sending a frisson of reaction through her body.

'*Fully* occupied!' she lied, glaring at him. 'Are you so vain as to believe that with these patients to tend and my father just out of Theatre, I'd be thinking of you?'

Kal smiled, a knowing smile that said he knew she'd lied, and that simple shifting of his lips and the glimpse of strong white teeth turned the frisson into a tremor.

'Your mother will let you know if anything goes wrong, and one of my family's jets is on standby should you need to fly home.'

Nell turned to him, the words not really making sense. Common sense while she was still frissoning and tremoring? And *one* of the jets? How many could one family have?

'A jet's on standby?'

Kal frowned at her.

'You're a guest in our country and doing a great service for us—greater than was originally intended. Of course we will see you get home as swiftly as possible, should it be necessary. I arranged for the crew to be on standby as soon as your mother phoned last night.'

I should thank him, Nell thought, but somehow the words wouldn't come. Being near Kal was confusing enough, battling the physical stuff even more debilitating, but kindness? No, she really couldn't handle kindness.

She forced her mind firmly back to the task in hand—first, deciding which patients were well enough for surgery, then working out treatment and procedures for the others.

They listed four patients for Theatre, then Kal headed off, as he'd be operating. Nell demonstrated to the nurses and junior medical staff how to gently slough off burned skin in the special bath. She then, with Yasmeen translating, reiterated all the information already given about barrier nursing, clean gowns and gloves, careful hand-washing—all the extreme measures staff had to take to prevent the spread of infection in the newly revealed wounds—and demonstrated how the spray-on dressing could be used to close them.

Her last patient was the man who'd been left for dead, and to her dismay he was no better. She'd been present when a specialist had checked his lungs, so she knew there was no damage, yet with only second-degree burns and with those only on about twelve per cent of his body, he should be picking up.

Was it because he had no family—he hadn't, as yet, been identified—that he was making so little progress?

Not even certain of his nationality, Nell still talked to him all the time she examined him, seeking the smallest sign of infection beneath the charred skin, checking his obs and test results again and again in search of some underlying problem that might explain his continuing decline.

In the end she knew no more and had to leave him with his nurse and make her way to the doctors' office. She was already late for her meeting with the dietitian to discuss the IV feeding of individual patients. The secretary someone had found for her translated the medical information on the computer from Arabic to English and, working with the dietitian and the computerised observations, patient weight and the urine and blood test results of each patient, they worked out the necessary nutritional needs for each individual.

'Should we change this daily?' the dietitian asked, and Nell shook her head.

'Maybe every second day, though if the obs show any deterioration in a patient's status I'll call you straight away.'

Two patients, they decided, could try oral feeding. Both had family support, and with encouragement should be able to manage the high calorie intake required to rebalance their bodies.

'No tea or coffee,' the dietitian reminded Nell. 'Just high-protein supplements for drinks. I'll write it up and make sure both the nurses and the kitchens understand.'

'And speak to the family members too, perhaps,' Nell suggested. 'They're the ones likely to bring in things that their relative might enjoy, without realising that everything he or she eats should be going towards their "good calorie" tally.'

The dietitian smiled as Nell put the two important words into inverted commas with her fingers.

'We do that, too,' she said, and Nell laughed, always pleased and surprised to find how little difference there was between her and the women with whom she now worked.

She felt the same bond with the physiotherapist and occupational therapist who followed the dietitian into the office. Both were aware the needs of burns patients differed from other hospitalised patients, but neither had had experience of dealing with them or of organising the special programmes they needed.

'It's important for us—the doctors—to watch for any change in the patient's sensory perception. Facial swelling can distort vision, or wounds might prevent patients wearing glasses or hearing aids, but we can miss things that the nurses or you therapists might pick up on, so be extra-vigilant.'

The young male physiotherapist assured Nell they would be, then asked questions about the advisability of patients exercising when they were in so much pain.

'The pain does make them reluctant to move any part of their bodies,' Nell agreed, conscious as she spoke that Kal had entered the room. 'But the wounds cause contractures so they need to exercise. Part of the problem with burns patients, more so than with, say, post-op patients, is irritability and agitation. This makes it harder to persuade them to try even gentle movement. Sometimes family members will help by encouraging the patient, but of course you then get the family member who tells you not to bother their son or brother, so you're battling on two fronts.'

They discussed the disorientation of patients in hospital and the necessity to always explain to the patient exactly what was happening. The OT would work with establishing good self-care routines with those well enough to undertake simple tasks for themselves, while the physio had a number of ideas for exercise that could suit even the most badly burned patients.

'You shouldn't have to be putting in extra time, teaching other people their jobs. Surely all the information is in their textbooks or on the internet,' Kal scolded. 'You're doing more than enough on the medical side.'

The secretary had departed with the two therapists, she to get some lunch for Nell and the other two to return to their jobs, so she and Kal were alone in the room. She looked at him as he sat down across the desk from her and tried to read his mood.

No chance! His face betrayed nothing, and the eyes that had once softened when he'd looked at her stared resolutely at a point somewhere beyond her left shoulder.

'The information *is* available, but if you haven't worked with burns patients before, you could be tentative, and the patients need certainty and firm, though caring handling. They've suffered a terrible psychological blow as well as the insult to their bodies, and need all the help they can get to make it through these initial stages of hospitalisation.'

She paused for a minute, thinking back over her early experience in burns.

'Actually, they need even more psychological support later, when they realise just how long term their treatment is going to be. There's no quick fix with burns, unfortunately. Speaking of which, how did the ops go?'

This is good, the voice in her head congratulated her. You stood up to Kal and now you're talking to him professional to professional, and hardly quaking at all inside.

'They went well,' he said, and Nell was sure he'd added a little prayer under his breath. But he was doing the 'professional to professional' business far better than she was. There was absolutely no indication in his face, or voice, or bearing, that last night he'd decreed they would be married, or that he'd then made her breathless with his love-making.

Love-making?

Unfortunately, while her head was querying the word he was speaking again, and she missed the first part. Something about the Spanish team.

'The team is made up of two plastic surgeons and two teams of theatre nurses. Naturally, they have more expertise in this field than I have, so although I want to learn whatever I can, I have to return to my own duties and my own surgical patients and will be here less often.'

Yes? And that means what? Nell was totally confused. Professional to professional was all well and good, but what about the personal issues yet to be resolved?

Was he being kind? Avoiding upsetting her further while she was concerned about her father's health?

Or did he intend to continue with this marriage idea and come to her apartment every night? Coolly professional by day, hot but emotionless lover at night?

Nell shuddered.

'Are you all right? Did you eat breakfast? Have you had lunch?'

Another switch in mood, but before Nell could reply, the secretary returned with Nell's lunch on a tray. The young woman bobbed a kind of bow to Kal, put down the tray and scampered away.

Nell was about to make a comment about the subservience many members of the staff showed him when he sighed.

'Ever since I started work at the hospital, it's been like that,' he said, his voice heavy with what sounded like genuine regret. 'I try to tell them that I'm just another doctor, but our people—the locals, not the staff who've come from other lands—still insist on some form of acknowledgement. It must have been bred into them with their mother's milk.'

He sighed again.

'Does it bother you so much that you sigh over it?' Nell asked, then realised it was hardly a professional-to-professional type question.

He looked directly at her, his usually alert gaze turned inward.

'Yes, it does,' he said then his eyes narrowed and he focussed on her. 'But, then, a lot of things bother me. Isn't it the case with everyone? You, for instance. Aren't you bothered by the fact you kept my son's life a secret from me for so long?'

The question was so unexpected, coming as it had when Nell had been lulled into a false sense of security by talk of work, that she couldn't answer it immediately. By the time she was ready to tell him that it wasn't a question that could be answered with a yes or no, he'd left the room, walking out as quietly as he'd walked in, leaving only his aura, haunting Nell like a wounded ghost.

A wounded ghost?

Hadn't she been just as wounded?

Don't start feeling sorry for him—he's hard as nails, as tough and deadly as the desert he loves so much.

She reached in her pocket for the card with the

phone number of her father's hospital on it. It would be evening at home, and right now what she needed was to touch base with her family. To ground herself with their voices—maybe even speak to her father if he was well enough. Then she'd phone home and talk to Patrick. Her family were her life—her reality. All this other stuff that was happening was like a story—something out of *Tales of the Arabian Nights*, only with darker overtones…

She picked at the pieces of cut fruit on the lunch tray as she waited for her call to go through to the hospital, then nibbled at some salad while she was put through to her mother.

'He's terrific—here, you can speak to him.'

Nell couldn't believe it. She knew people came out of major surgery far better these days, but to be able to speak to her father when he was less than twenty-four hours post-op?

'Dad!'

'I'm fine, honey. Tired but fine. Patrick came by earlier. He's looking good. He was in great spirits because he'd cut his hair.'

Her mother took the phone and explained how delighted Patrick had been to have enough hair to cut it back to a number one—the favoured, almost shaved look all his friends wore.

It was such a normal, innocuous conversation, Nell smiled. Yes, family definitely grounded one! They talked some more about nothing in particular, then said goodbye, Nell assuring her mother she was looking after herself.

It wasn't until she'd hung up that Nell realised there'd

been no mention of Kal. Was her mother being tactful or had the conversation she'd had with Kal meant little to her?

Not that it mattered, although Nell felt a little niggle that her mother hadn't said it had been nice to talk to him or asked how he was—asked anything…

'What do you mean, I've no operations scheduled?'

Kal wasn't exactly yelling at his secretary, but his voice was probably a little louder than it needed to be.

'You were busy with the accident victims and I assumed you would be for some time, so when Dr Armstrong offered to do your list, I checked with all the patients to see if any of them minded, and they didn't, so he's operating here today and again tomorrow.'

She looked doubtfully at him.

'I could tell him you're free to do tomorrow's list, but then he might think—'

'That I think he's not competent,' Kal grumbled. 'Which isn't the case at all! He's a top surgeon—we've worked together often.'

Telling his secretary something she already knew! Of course she wouldn't have thought twice when Bob Armstrong had made the offer. The pair of them worked as a team on complex cases a couple of times a month.

None of this made him feel any better.

'So what am I supposed to do?' he demanded.

'Go back to the burns unit?' The tentative suggestion made him scowl. Working close to Nell was having an exceedingly detrimental effect on him, turning him into a person he didn't like at all, while at the same time it was giving him thoughts he shouldn't have—thoughts about how soon he could get her back into bed.

Never!

He was so certain he'd blown his chances with Nell that he felt depressed.

But thinking of Nell gave him an idea.

'I'll take a day off,' he announced, and his secretary looked so startled you'd have thought he'd suggested he was taking up needlework.

'But you had a day off last week,' she protested, her voice faint with shock.

'And two days off in how long—six months? Is that too much to ask?'

'Of course not.' She was scrabbling to recover her composure. 'Of course it isn't. I'm always telling you you should take more days off. It's just…'

'Unusual?' Kal offered helpfully, then he decided this conversation had gone on long enough. 'I'll see the Spanish team before I leave, and make sure they're settled into their accommodations and have everything they need. After that, I'll be contactable on my mobile.'

He walked out of the room, wanting privacy. Then he'd see his hospital administrator and give him the task of looking after the Spaniards. God or Fate or some kindly juxtaposition of the planets had given him this free time and he wasn't going to waste it. He was going to Australia to get his son…

The pretty, suntanned blonde at the car-hire counter in the main airport terminal building laughed when he said he hadn't been in Brisbane for fourteen years.

'You'll find it very different—especially the volume of traffic—but there's a street directory in the car so you should be able to find your way.'

She handed him the keys, explained where the car was parked and wished him luck.

Not that he needed it. The roads were still familiar and he drove to the Roberts' house with only one wrong turn. It was late afternoon and no one was at home, but he was content to sit on the front steps of the neat brick house with its wide, tree-shaded verandas and think about the past—about waiting here for Nell—until someone returned.

Mrs Roberts? Or the aunt called Mary? Kal couldn't recall her but, then, Nell had had a multitude of relations. Perhaps that had been part of what had attracted him to her—because her sense of family was as strong as his.

Family!

He really hoped it would be Patrick who came first, but when he thought of Patrick—of this stranger who was his son—his heart crunched into a tight hard lump.

Instead he had thought of Mrs Roberts again. She'd always been kind and welcoming—both of Nell's parents had been. The fact he was of a different race and culture had meant nothing to them, content that Nell was happy with him, pleased to think he could give her happiness.

'For one whole year!'

He spat the words out bitterly, wondering at the arrogance of his young self who'd outlined the 'rules' of the relationship to Nell, telling her from the beginning it would only be an affair.

Later, loving her, he'd explained why. Explained the pact he'd made with his parents. He could break tradition by studying medicine—even do a year's post-graduate study in far-away Australia—but he'd promised he'd then return and marry in the traditional way, marry the wife he didn't know but to whom he'd been betrothed since he'd been sixteen.

'Hi! Can I help you? Are you looking for my grand-parents? I'm afraid Gramps is in hospital at the moment and Gran's up there, making sure the nurses look after him properly.'

The tall young lad had stopped a couple of feet in front of Kal, who stared at him, shaken, bewildered and tongue-tied as he drank in his son's appearance. Anger that this should be his first meeting stirred turbulence into an overwhelming rush of emotion at seeing him.

'Aunt Mary should be home soon. She said she'd do a run up to the hospital with some clean clothes and stuff, so I guess that's where she is.'

There was another awkward pause, the result of Kal's continued inability to speak, then the boy stuck out his hand.

'I'm Patrick, anyway.'

Kal stood up and took the hand offered to him, feel-ing the fragile bones in the thin fingers, knowing the boy's lanky leanness was a sign of recent illness, not a growth spurt. More anger rushed through him. He should have known—he should have been here! What if his son had died?

Realising he was probably freaking the boy out with his silence, he blotted the anger from his mind, swal-lowed hard and introduced himself.

'Kal,' he said, with gentle pressure on the bony fin-gers. 'I'm Kal.'

'My father's name is Kal,' Patrick said cautiously. 'His whole name is Khalil al Kalada—he's a kind of prince in a foreign country.'

The stream of information stopped abruptly and the boy stared at Kal, his gaze going from the top of Kal's head, down to his feet, then back up again. Then the colour drained from the lad's face, and Kal reached out to grab him, scared the shock might prove too much.

But Patrick stepped away, straightening his shoulders, and though Kal could see the tremors in his son's limbs and the dryness of the lips Patrick licked and licked again, he didn't touch him—just waited—and watched the realisation dawning across the teenager's face.

'You're him, aren't you?'

Patrick stared at him, as if transfixed, but try as he might, searching desperately through his muddled mind, Kal could find no words to say, his throat closed tight with emotion, his mind focussed on this tall, gangly youth with eyes the colour of good brandy.

The boy recovered first.

'Does Mum know you're here? Is this OK? Did she ask you to come? Send you? Is it OK to be talking to you? I don't know the rules about this kind of stuff.'

He rubbed his hands on the sides of his shorts, as if embarrassment had made them sweat, then he grinned at Kal, though his eyes were filmed with tears and there was a suspicious tremble on his pale lips.

'Sorry, but Mum's never got up to what to do when I meet my dad, not in any of the talks she's given me. But I know some Arabic.'

He put his hands together in front of him and greeted his father with the traditional words his tutor had taught him.

'Salaam alaikum.'

Peace be with you.

Kal tried to speak but couldn't. His chest was bound tight with emotion, his voice lost somewhere in the tidal wave of love that had swept over him when this Australian boy had greeted him in his own tongue.

He shook his head and stepped closer to his son, putting his arms around the boy, hugging him tightly and holding him, feeling the trembling tension in the too-thin frame, feeling it slowly abate and the boy's body slump against his.

His own emotion broke like a wave on a rocky shore, flooding in then sweeping back, leaving him drained and depleted.

Then Patrick broke away and looked at him.

'You *are* him, aren't you?' Then he frowned. 'Look, I know it's rude, but should you show me something saying who you are? You see, I should ask you in—will ask you in—but stranger danger and all that stuff…'

Overwhelmingly proud of this boy-man, Kal pulled his passport out of his pocket and handed it to Patrick.

'You're right to be cautious,' he finally managed to say, while in another part of his mind gratitude to Nell for raising Patrick so well momentarily blotted out the anger he felt towards her for depriving him of so much.

Patrick looked at the photo in the passport, then at the man who stood before him. Kal felt his scrutiny and grew anxious that further inspection might stop the boy from liking him. But all Patrick did was rub his finger gently over the photo a few times, then he looked up at Kal and said, 'This is so weird, meeting like this. I didn't think we ever would meet, you see. Not after Mum explained about your other wife and everything. I've never blamed you. I understood. Maybe, when I was a kid and went to things like soccer and a lot of the other boys had dads there and I only had Mum and Gramps, I'd think about it, but Mum told me about your promise and I understood that things were different where you lived and promises and honour and all that stuff were really important to you.'

Kal turned away so the boy wouldn't see the tears in his eyes. Was it going to be like this all the time? Would everything the boy said overwhelm him with emotion?

And what of Nell? Could he continue to be angry with a woman who had produced a teenager with so much guts and understanding?

By God, he could!

'So if you want to come in?'

He'd missed the first part of the invitation but, still holding the passport, Patrick was now walking up the front steps.

Seeing the passport reminded Kal of why he was here. Enough of this sentimentalism—it was time to be practical.

'Do you have a passport?' he asked, and Patrick, who'd reached the veranda, turned to smile at him.

'Of course. I got one a couple of years ago when I went to New Zealand with the soccer team. Before I got sick.'

He stopped suddenly and frowned.

'I suppose you *have* talked to Mum, and that's why you're here.' His frown deepened and for the first time Kal saw a resemblance to Nell—perhaps because just about all she'd done recently had been to frown at him! 'I talked to her after she phoned the hospital last night and she didn't say anything about you coming, but she'd probably have been upset about Gramps.'

Kal shook his head. Love, wonder, anger, love—far too many emotions for one man to handle, but the boy was waiting for an answer.

'I explained to your grandmother when I spoke to

her. It seemed a good idea, with your grandfather recovering from the operation and your grandmother being busy for a while looking after him, for you to come and visit me. After all, your mother's over there. So what do you think?'

Patrick stared at him, delight warring with doubt in his open face.

'I don't know about leaving Gran,' he said, putting the doubt into words first.

'Your grandmother thought it was an excellent idea, but you shouldn't take my word for it. I can take you up to the hospital to see them both and you can ask them what they think.'

The doubt gave way to tentative excitement.

'Would I be able to see your falcons?' Patrick asked, then, before Kal could answer this totally unexpected question, he darted away, returning seconds later with a book he pressed into Kal's hands.

'It's my favourite book—well, almost favourite. I've got so many it's hard to choose but I read this one again and again.'

Kal looked at it, his fingers tracing the title—*The History of the Sport of Falconry*—unconsciously echoing his son's movement on the passport.

'Did your mother give you this?' It took a while but he finally managed to force the words out through his tightened vocal cords.

'Of course. She said it was your favourite sport—better even than soccer—so I thought I should learn about it, just in case…'

'You ever met me?'

Tears filmed the boy's eyes again, and Kal saw his

son's Adam's apple bob as he swallowed hard, but he couldn't speak either, so once again he hugged his son, the book squashed between their bodies.

This time he broke away.

'Go and pack—the weather's warm. Will you need schoolbooks? Do you have any important exams coming up?'

Patrick seemed to welcome the shift in conversation, and grinned.

'Schoolbooks? No way! I've missed so much school, this year is a catch-up year and I'm repeating a lot of work I've already done. Mum says if I find any of it a struggle, she'll get a tutor, but I've just done a chemistry test and I think I did OK.'

He disappeared into the back part of the house, returning seconds later.

'I'm sorry—would you like a cup of tea or something to eat?'

Kal had to smile. Mrs Roberts had always welcomed him to this house like that.

'No, I'm fine,' he told Patrick, and as the boy turned away again Kal looked around, feeling unaccountably at home in this house he hadn't visited for fourteen years.

Patrick returned within minutes, a huge canvas bag slung across his shoulders.

'I hope this isn't too much?' he said, the anxiety in his voice betraying his youth and a desire to please.

'Not at all,' Kal assured him. 'You've got your toothbrush?'

'Actually no.'

The bag dropped to the floor, making a dull thud that suggested much of the contents were books, and Patrick disappeared once more, reappearing with a sheepish expression and a tartan toiletries bag.

'Haven't got my tablets either.'

He headed for the kitchen and pulled a plastic container down from a high shelf. Then, as if struck by a sudden thought, he turned to Kal.

'I know you're a doctor—do you know about the leukaemia? Know I have to have blood tests all the time?'

The question was so matter-of-factly asked that Kal choked with emotion again.

'We'll do the tests,' he managed to assure his son, then the two of them left the house, Patrick running back inside to leave a note for Mary, then locking the front door and bounding down the steps with barely a backward glance.

CHAPTER FIVE

'HE'S doing what?' Nell yelled into the phone, unable to believe what her mother was telling her.

'I thought you knew. He said he'd talked to you about it—about it being a good opportunity to meet Patrick and get to know him while you were over there—and to be honest, Nell, I thought it would be for the best. It's far better for Patrick not to be around while your dad convalesces.'

That made sense, but the effrontery of the man, to go flying off to Australia without so much as a by your leave and pick up *her* son and fly back here with him.

The hide of him!

'Nell?'

Her mother's anxiety travelled over the thousands of kilometres between them and, hearing it, Nell hastened to reassure her that, of course, she'd done the right thing in letting Patrick go with Kal and, of course, it would be better for Patrick, and probably much easier on everyone to have him out of the house.

But where did that leave her? She all but whimpered as she put down the phone, then anger swamped the panic. That manipulative man! Taking off like that, kidnapping her son and presenting the whole deal as a *fait accompli*.

And he'd lied to her—telling her he had to return to the surgical ward and his surgery duties, and flying off to Australia instead.

Consumed by rage, Nell paced the apartment and though she told herself it would be good to see Patrick, an uneasy fear overlay even that small glimmer of pleasure.

Fear?

She stopped pacing, wanting to explore this new emotion further, but the phone interrupted her.

'Mum! It's Patrick. I'm ringing from Kal's jet. Just like you phoned me from the plane on your flight. Kal said to tell you we're due to land at about ten in the morning your time, and he'll bring me straight to the apartment at the hospital. Isn't this exciting?'

As exciting as walking on broken glass with bare feet or swallowing fire! Nell thought, but the joy in Patrick's voice stopped her saying anything negative. He'd been through so much and had had precious little to be excited about lately. What she had to say would be said to Kal. It would keep!

'It will be lovely to see you,' she said lamely, then added a goodbye and hung up. No need now to think about where the fear had come from—it had found a focus. 'Kal's jet', 'Kal said'—oh, yes, the fear was that this man would steal her son. Not only physically, as he'd done already, but emotionally—and then where would she be?

Fuming with frustration that she couldn't immediately tackle Kal about his duplicity, she took another turn around the room, then realised just how clever he had been. She couldn't tackle him in front of Patrick, or do or say anything to make Patrick think what Kal had done was wrong. No, right from the start, she'd been determined that Patrick should grow up thinking his father was an honourable man—bound by his promises and beliefs.

How could she betray that conviction now?

Back and forth she marched, her mind in turmoil, though now one small ray of light shone tentatively in the darkness. Patrick's presence would prevent Kal seducing her with his touch and kisses—there'd be no more passionate love-making in either of their beds.

Contrarily, this thought didn't bring the solace it should have, so she went back to being angry with the man's behaviour as far as Patrick was concerned.

She was at the furthest point from the phone when it rang again. Thinking this time it might be Kal himself—with an explanation or even an apology—she shot across the room and grabbed it.

'It's the burns unit, Dr Warren. Could you come?'

Nell didn't hesitate. Whoever had rung might not have had enough knowledge of English to explain why Nell was needed, but she knew she wouldn't have been disturbed as she glanced at her watch one in the morning if it wasn't an emergency.

She met Yasmeen, who had also been summoned, in the corridor outside the ward.

'It's your man—the one we can't identify,' Yasmeen said to her. 'BP dropping, oxygen sats in his blood right down—he's dying, Nell.'

'He can't die!' Nell stormed, pleased to have an outlet for her anger. 'Not now.'

Yasmeen said nothing, and Nell understood. These people accepted death with far more composure than she could. As far as they were concerned, death was simply an extension of life and the timing of it was the will of God.

The man was comatose but, then, he'd never been more than semi-conscious at any time since he'd been in hospital. Or as far as they knew, he hadn't. Unable to speak because of the tracheostomy, they had encouraged him to respond with movements of his hands or eyelids, or by writing on a pad they had tied to his bed, but no matter what language they used to speak to him, there'd been no sign that he heard or understood.

'He has to have some underlying illness!' Nell said. 'We've been testing his blood but only to see what's happening inside him, not for any signs of disease. He's got oxygen flowing into his lungs through the tracheostomy tube, his red blood cell count has been OK—not marvellous but not terrible—so why aren't those cells picking up oxygen? Is it a disease that destroys their carrying capacity? Is that what we're missing?'

She was thinking out loud and didn't expect Yasmeen to answer, but the other woman was staring at her as if she'd asked a million-dollar question. Silence for a moment, then Yasmeen smiled—the kind of smile that went with a million-dollar answer.

'Maybe all along he had heart problems. Maybe he has some kind of transposition of the arteries—only not a total transposition but the pulmonary veins aren't feeding their oxygen-rich blood back into the heart for some reason…'

'Not arteries but valve problems—a leaky valve.' Nell felt as if a bright light had been turned on. 'The oxygenated blood is slipping back and being recirculated through the lungs.' She thought about the function of the heart for a moment, then shook her head.

'No, that wouldn't work. But it could be some kind of hole between the ventricular septums. Maybe he had weakness there that has worsened with age. Didn't you, or Kal, or someone, tell me that the ex-pats' hospital was getting a wonderful reputation for its success with heart patients and people were flying in from all over the world to be treated? Heart disease and cardiac surgery—two things for which the hospitals here are famous!'

Yasmeen nodded, then walked across to the desk and lifted the phone. She turned towards Nell, obviously thinking, then put down the receiver without dialling.

'There won't be anyone there at this time of night who can help us, but we should phone first thing in the morning and ask if they were expecting a patient for a heart operation. In the meantime, what do we do?'

'Get hold of a heart specialist. Do you have one here or do your heart patients go to the other hospital?'

'We've got consultants who work here, but…'

Yasmeen hesitated.

'You don't like calling them out at night? Too bad,' Nell said. 'You can blame the crazy Australian doctor. Let's get someone here to take a look at our man. In the meantime, I'm going to increase the oxygen flow. Some oxygen is getting into his blood. Maybe with a higher concentration, enough will get through to keep him going until we find out what's wrong.'

Yasmeen went back to the phone, and Nell returned to her patient's bedside. She didn't know why this man had become so important to her, but she had no intention of giving up on him now, or letting him give up either.

She adjusted the flow meter, checked his IV lines, speaking firmly to him about hanging on all the time, telling him he owed it to his family, although she didn't know if he had one. Certainly no one had come forth to claim him, although by now details of this so-called mystery man had probably been printed in newspapers all around the world.

But if Yasmeen thought calling in a consultant in the early hours of the morning had been a bad idea, the consultant himself thought it an even worse idea, though he apparently—he communicated only with Yasmeen—considered their tentative diagnosis a possibility and agreed to do an exploratory cardiac catheterisation in the morning.

Glaring at Nell, he said something more to Yasmeen then departed, leaving Yasmeen to explain the situation to Nell.

'Bother the man!' Nell muttered. 'He was here—already awake—so why couldn't he do it now?'

'He needs equipment and staff,' Yasmeen said lamely, and it was Nell's turn to glare.

'You're telling me someone else might be using the equipment now? And what staff? A radiographer to follow the progress of the tube up into the heart? Surely there's a radiographer on duty.'

She was about to say more, but noticed Yasmeen's look of distress and realised she was taking out her own bad temper on the woman who'd been nothing but helpful since they'd first met. She put her arm around Yasmeen's shoulders and gave her a hug.

'I'm sorry, it's not your fault. And now that we've at least got something organised to happen, why don't you go back to bed? I'm happy to stay here with him. In fact, there are a few things I want to check on some other patients, so I might as well be here.'

Yasmeen argued but in the end she relented, but it was only after she'd gone that Nell wondered whether she lived in the hospital apartments or had to travel some distance to her home.

In fact, she knew nothing whatsoever about Yasmeen, except that she was an excellent doctor and her English had an American accent. Was it that the accident and doing the best she could for so many patients had made Nell incurious, or was it because Kal occupied all the spare edges of her mind so there were no brain cells left for normal musings about a colleague's life?

Tomorrow she'd find out more about Yasmeen. No, tomorrow had already become today and today Patrick would arrive, flown in by his father in a private jet. Damn Kal! What thirteen-year-old kid could fail to be impressed by such a display of wealth and power?

Nell's patient stirred, saving her further anguish as she concentrated on the readouts on the monitor. The increased oxygen flow wasn't helping and the drugs she'd given him to raise his blood pressure had lifted it slightly, but not enough to give her hope that he was improving. The young nurse who was specialling the man said something, and Nell, looking at her, realised the girl was praying. She had taken the man's hand, carefully holding it so she didn't touch the burn wounds on his wrist, and now her head was bent towards it and soft, liquid words slipped from her lips.

Nell remembered Kal telling her that his people had always used prayer as a part of the healing process. They had remedies for illnesses, but every cure, even in these days of modern medicine, was offered along with prayer, for was it not God's will that the patient lived or died?

Could prayer do what medicine couldn't? Nell wondered, turning her attention back to the monitor.

No change, but the young nurse's faith touched Nell, and she sank down in the chair on the other side of the bed and added her own quiet prayer for the man's recovery.

Together they watched over him through the remainder of the night, and by morning, Nell was pleased to see, he had picked up slightly, so when the consultant returned, Yasmeen was able to report that the patient was well enough for him to do the cardiac catheterisation and, if it looked possible, even to try a balloon valvuplasty to close the defective septum.

'*If* there is a defective septum,' Nell muttered to herself, certain the solution to her patient's problems couldn't be that easy.

But it was, and the surgeon emerged from the small operating theatre so triumphant he forgot he'd been pretending not to speak English. He gave her an inch-by-inch description of his masterful catheterisation, then detailed the skill he'd shown in fixing the defective wall, finishing with the intimation that if the patient didn't improve now, it would be Nell's fault, not his.

Nell thanked him and followed the wardsmen wheeling the patient back to the unit. Tiredness was swamping her now, dragging at her feet so she felt as if she walked through mud, but her mind was on the man—wondering what changes she should now make to his treatment, considering possible reactions between the drugs the heart consultant had prescribed and the antibiotic and pain-relief regime he was on for his burns.

'Nell!'

The sound of her name, spoken as if it was being repeated, made her turn, and there, ten metres behind her in the corridor, was Kal.

Kal!

Patrick!

'Where's Patrick?' she demanded, too tired and confused to even begin to say all the other things she wanted to say to this man.

'He's in your apartment. I left him there and came to find you. I'd have thought you would have been waiting for him.'

The slight hint of reproof in Kal's voice was enough. Nell took off down the corridor, fury blotting out her surroundings and making her want to strike out at this man who was turning her life upside down.

'How dare you speak to me like that?' she raged, lifting her fists to pound them on his chest, only to have him seize them in his hands. 'And how dare you sneak off and take my child? Of all the underhanded, horrible things to do, and while I'm here working at *your* hospital!'

'He's my child, too,' Kal reminded her, his voice as hard and smooth as steel, his hands imprisoning her struggling fists with effortless ease. 'And if we're talking underhanded or horrible, wouldn't keeping him from me for thirteen years fit that description?'

'I *couldn't* tell you!' Nell snapped. 'Do you think I didn't want to? Wouldn't have given anything to have you back? But at least I acted from honour! Something you pretended to uphold. Honour! Ha!' she scoffed. 'Was this honourable behaviour, Sheik Kalada, sneaking off behind my back? Taking my child?'

'Our child!'

And at that moment she hated him. Hated him as much as she had loved him. Because he was right! Patrick was *their* child.

'It was still the wrong thing to do!' she muttered, hanging onto the anger as this proximity to Kal, his grip, less tight now on her fists, was turning wrath to attraction.

'It was wrong, but would you have agreed without a

lengthy argument?' he asked quietly. 'It turned out a friend had taken my surgery list so I had time to go and come back. Your mother seemed relieved that Patrick would be out of the way while your father convalesced, and it's not as if you were in some other country. I flew out to Australia to bring Patrick to back to be with his mother.'

The effrontery of this bald-faced lie pushed attraction aside.

'You brought him back for your own reasons,' Nell stormed, 'so don't make out like it was some Scout good deed for the day.'

She snatched her hands out of his and stormed away, intending to go straight to the apartment but aware she'd have to hide the anger she was feeling. Patrick would be excited by his adventure and think it was the greatest fun for all of them to be together. She couldn't dash that excitement or throw a dark cloud of gloom over his delight.

'Nell, Nell!'

Yasmeen's voice followed her up the corridor, and she turned back to see the other woman explaining something to Kal, her hands moving swiftly as if demonstrating what was happening, her face, even at a distance, anguished.

Nell hurried back.

'It's your man,' Yasmeen told her. 'His BP's dropped again—dropped drastically.'

'Damn!' Nell muttered, and headed off with swift strides back towards the ward. She sensed Kal following, and was reminded of where things stood. She stopped and turned.

'Kal, I have to go to this patient. Could you explain to Patrick?'

Kal looked at her and for the first time saw the grey

tinge of exhaustion in her usually clear skin and the dark circles under her eyes.

'Have you slept at all?' he demanded, and she found a small smile to offer him. The kind of valiant smile that made his heart ache.

'Not recently,' she said, then she touched him on the arm. 'But I have to go and I can't leave Patrick on his own.'

Her fingers tightened on his muscle, and she looked into his eyes as she added, 'Please?'

Of course he'd go to the boy! So why was he hesitating? Why was he making this woman almost beg?

Guilt, compunction and an overwhelming sense of emotion he was sure couldn't possibly be love swept over him. He leant forward and, ignoring Yasmeen, who'd been standing beside Nell, obviously fascinated by the byplay, kissed Nell gently on the cheek.

'I'll take care of Patrick,' he promised. Then he walked away before he could hug her and apologise for all the things that had gone wrong between them since they'd met again, and tell her how wonderful their son was and congratulate her...

She'd disappeared from view by the time he got that far in the list of things he wanted to say, and he hauled his mind back, reminding it that what she'd done had been wrong—that he was the injured party here, and she the one who should be apologising.

He went back to Nell's apartment, ready to explain the emergency. As a doctor's son, Patrick would surely understand. But he didn't have to explain anything. The lad was stretched out the couch, sound asleep, although the television was on, blaring out some rock video.

Kal studied him, seeing resemblances to himself and

to his brother's children. Not much of Nell. Had it worried her that her son was so much *his* child in looks? She'd obviously been at such pains to ensure Patrick never thought badly of the father who'd deserted them, he doubted she'd have worried much about his looks.

Kal went into the kitchen and poured himself a glass of cold water. He should go to work—check out what was happening, not only on the ward but in the hospital as a whole. But he wouldn't leave Patrick on his own. Even had he wanted to, he'd promised Nell, so he picked up the phone and called his secretary, explained where he was and checked on what was happening.

'We can survive without you for a few hours—or even days,' she reminded him. 'That's why you chose good deputies. You've just never believed they could run things as well as you do. Have faith.'

Kal smiled at her admonishments, but he'd been brought up to take responsibility, not only for his own actions but for his people. It was a hard habit to break.

He noticed the pile of books Patrick had unpacked and stacked on Nell's dining-room table. A few more piles and the apartment would look like his. He picked out the one on falconry and sat down to read, smiling when he saw the fine marks Patrick had made beside some passages and the star he'd put against Kal's grandfather's name. Yes, the boy's great-grandfather had been a master in training birds, and this had obviously appealed to the lad.

Nell returned to the ward, where the registrar and a junior doctor were already by the bed.

'Has the heart consultant been called?' she asked Yasmeen, taking in the grey, depleted look of her patient.

'He's on his way,' the registrar replied, and Nell nodded at him. He was always happy to try out his English on her.

The first place Nell checked was the area of the groin where the catheter had been inserted, but though the dressing showed some blood, there wasn't enough to explain the man's condition.

'Internal bleeding seems the most likely scenario for such a sudden collapse,' she said. 'We need a scan. Will the registrar have to order it or—'

But at that stage, with not even a sigh or murmur of protest, the man stopped breathing while the monitor showed his heart had stopped.

'Resuscitation?' the young doctor asked, and Nell considered it—thought about the shock paddles, the man's injured body leaping on the bed—and rejected the option with regret. Even when he had seemed conscious, the man had shown no will to live, and though she'd fought for him and urged him to fight, it had been plain he hadn't wanted to undertake the battle.

Sheer stubbornness on her part had kept him alive, but now she wasn't going to push him further.

Her explanations for this decision, however, should be medical, not emotional, and she said quietly, 'If we shock his heart and the leak is in there, or in the vessel the specialist used in the catheterisation, all we're doing is pumping more blood into his body cavity, giving the lungs even less room to expand. Instead of saving him, we'd be killing him again.'

The others nodded, seemingly satisfied with her theory, but her heart ached with the loss of this man she didn't know, and she stayed in the room when the others left, helping the nurse prepare him for his move to the mortuary. She'd like him autopsied but didn't know if that would be done as a matter of routine for all deaths in hospitals in this country. She'd have to ask—

Kal. She no longer had an excuse not to go to Patrick, but Kal would be there, and the thought of seeing the two of them together—father and son—was almost too much for her to contemplate.

She found Yasmeen instead and asked her about autopsies.

'It should be done,' Yasmeen said worriedly, 'but—'

The heart consultant appeared out of the doctor's office and Nell understood the 'but'.

'I've signed the death certificate. Given the seriousness of his burns, it's no wonder he died. It really was a waste of time my operating. No need for us to do an autopsy.'

He was so certain—*and* so obnoxious—Nell dug in her heels.

'His family might want details. They might ask for a full report.'

'He has no family,' the consultant told her.

'Of course he has—we just haven't found them yet.'

Yasmeen was tugging nervously at Nell's arm but Nell found it was good to be getting rid of a bit of accumulated ire on this man.

'And when we do, how do we explain?'

'He died of burn injuries,' the man snapped, then he strode away.

'Can we go above his head?' Nell was aware she was being stubborn but she still asked Yasmeen the question.

'Only to Kal. The man's a consultant so he's not a hospital employee, but Kal still decides what does and doesn't happen in the hospital. You could phone his office.'

Nell nodded, although she knew, unless Patrick was being inducted into the running of a hospital, the CEO wouldn't be in his office but in her apartment.

'I'll track him down but, in the meantime, can we hold the man's body somewhere? I don't want action being taken on the death certificate just yet.'

'We have to hold him anyway and keep trying to find his family,' Yasmeen reminded her, 'although if he's of our faith he should be buried within twenty-four hours.'

She was frowning, as if the complications were too much for her, and Nell put her arm around her.

'Kal will sort it out,' she said, and though she was still so angry she could spit over Kal's behaviour, she had faith that he would indeed sort it out.

She gave Yasmeen a hug and departed, assuming Kal would still be with Patrick in her apartment. But the skip of excitement her heart gave at the thought of seeing her son was soon damped down by memories of her patient's death.

'I should have thought of heart problems,' she said, talking in a low but anguished tone to Kal. They were in the kitchen of her apartment and, having feasted her eyes on her sleeping son and assured herself he had good colour in his cheeks, she'd drawn Kal into the kitchen to explain the problem. 'But even so, once we realised it, we should have been able to save him.'

The anger she felt towards him had softened when he'd taken her hand then put his arm around her shoulders as he'd told her how sorry he was that the man who meant so much to her had died.

'There was no reason for you to think of heart problems,' Kal now assured her. 'Look, the man had a pad on which to write. He was conscious enough some of the time to have responded to questions, and we'd asked him in—what?—a dozen languages if he had any underlying health problems. And he heard the questions because he looked away when we asked them—ignoring us.'

Kal turned her to face him, and tucked a lock of hair behind her ear.

'No one could have done more for him. Remember, if you hadn't stopped to check him, he'd have been delivered to the mortuary that first day.'

Disturbed by Kal's gentleness and also by the abatement of her anger, Nell backed away.

'Can we have him autopsied?'

Kal thought for a minute.

'Why?'

'I don't think he died of his burns. I think he haemorrhaged internally, possibly as a result of the operation.'

'As a result of the consultant's carelessness? Is that what you're saying?'

'No. The man is probably a very competent surgeon, but if it was a mistake, shouldn't we know about it? Doesn't the patient deserve that much from us?'

Kal shrugged, but his reply was less casual.

'Yes, he does. We'll autopsy him. If nothing else, finding the cause of death might save the hospital problems later should some family member turn up.'

Nell was pleased but knew someone who wouldn't be so excited. For a moment she considered not saying anything, but knew it wouldn't be fair to embroil Kal unknowingly in a problem.

'The heart consultant is against it.'

Kal raised an eyebrow as if to say, So? and Nell had to smile. The arrogant Kal was back.

But her smile faded as she remembered it was the arrogant man she needed to fight—the Kal who'd gone out to Australia and, without her permission, taken her son out of the country. She was reasonably certain there were illegalities involved, although she had no intention of pursuing them.

No, it was the principle of the thing that was bothering her.

'The boy's awake.'

From the warning note in Kal's voice he'd guessed what she was thinking, and frustration with the situation meant she had to force a smile as she turned towards her son. But the pretence didn't last long. Seeing him, hearing his happy shout of 'Mum' and feeling his long, thin body in her arms as he hugged her fiercely brushed away all her anger.

'This *is* a surprise,' she said finally, holding him at arm's length so she could look at him. 'Did you remember your tablets? Did you think to phone the hospital to get them to send your records?'

She saw the happiness in his face fade slightly and gave him another hug.

'Of course you didn't. How could you think of everything with Gramps in hospital and with your…with Kal whisking you away in his plane? It's OK. I can email them to send the files direct to me and I'll print them out for whichever doctor your…Kal chooses for you while you're here.'

Beyond Patrick's shoulder she saw Kal's scowl. Was he annoyed because she couldn't bring herself to say the word 'father' or because she'd intimated this was only a short visit?

But of course it was—so he'd better not be thinking any different.

She scowled right back at him, then wondered if she'd guessed wrongly when he said to Patrick, 'I think it's time you tasted local food. Your mother's been up all night but I doubt if she's eaten, so how about you go off and forage?' He dug in his pocket and drew out a roll of notes, peeled off several and handed them to Patrick. 'If you go down to the ground floor in the elevator and turn right, you can't miss the canteen. It's self-service so choose a few plates of whatever looks good, put them on a tray, bring them back up and we'll share it.'

Patrick looked as if Kal had given him a gift rather than a job to get him out of the way.

'Will they have felafel? And hummus? And shish kebabs? And Mum does a fruity kind of rice as well, but I forget its name.'

'Go check it out,' Kal said to him, leading the way to the door then standing there while Patrick strode towards the elevator.

'He's a fine boy,' he said, coming back towards Nell, his eyes and the gravity in his voice making the words even stronger praise. 'You've done a wonderful job with him. I'd like—'

'I don't want your compliments on Patrick's upbringing,' Nell snorted, although she'd gone just a little teary to hear Kal say those words. 'I want an explanation for your behaviour, and I want to know what you intend doing now you've disrupted Patrick's life like this.'

Kal stiffened, drawing himself up to his full height and looking down at her with hard, unyielding eyes.

'I intend to get to know my son, and then, when I judge he will be easy with them, I intend to introduce him to my family.'

'Introduce him to your family?' Nell knew her words were faint, but so was she. 'You'd introduce him? Acknowledge him?'

'He is my son!' Kal said, his voice as cold as wind off snow. 'They are his family. Of course he should know them.'

Nell felt for the chair she knew was somewhere behind her, pulled it out from the table and sat down with a bump.

This is what you want, she reminded herself. OK, it hasn't happened as you planned, but if they meet Patrick surely they'll all be willing to be tested as possible bone-marrow donors.

But if they meet Patrick…

Her mind tried to grasp the ramifications—to work out where this family reunion might lead. Surely Kal couldn't think Patrick could stay on in this country. It had been all very well for Kal to have talked of conditions—and even, ridiculously, of marriage—but Nell's life was back in Australia, and Patrick's place was with her.

Her heart scrunched with momentary panic.

Wasn't it?

CHAPTER SIX

'WHAT would you like? A cup of tea? Coffee? Have you had anything at all to eat? Don't you know about looking after yourself?'

Kal's voice was brusque, but as Nell shook her head in answer to any or all of his questions, she was relieved he thought her sudden subsidence into the chair was to do with hunger or over-tiredness.

Although now, with Patrick gone, she should be talking to him about this family idea he'd suddenly dumped on her.

He beat her to it, but with talk of her family, not his.

'I saw your father. I took Patrick to the hospital before we left. He—your father—looked remarkably well and the doctors are apparently delighted with his recovery.'

Pleased by this diversion, Nell looked up at the man looming over her.

'And Mum? How's she holding up?'

Kal smiled—the warm, genuine, lighting-up-his-face smile that had always made Nell's heart race.

And still did.

'She's exactly as she always was. A spaceship could land in her back yard and as the little yellow and purple spotted aliens poured out, she'd greet them with a smile and offer tea or coffee. She's sitting up there by your father, knitting brightly coloured scarves, and has a large bag of wool so the nurses can choose what colour scarf they'd like her to knit them. Needless to say, she has them eating out her hand and they can't do enough for your father.'

Nell had to smile. Yes, that was her mum!

And though she'd cut out her tongue rather than admit it, Nell knew that not having to worry about Patrick with his meals and tests and doctors' appointments would ease the strain on her mother right through her father's convalescence.

'So, with your family all tidied away, that leaves us,' Kal said.

'There is no us,' Nell reminded him. 'There's you, there's me and there's Patrick. And now you've finessed him here, you can get to know him, but you'd better be able to take some time off work to keep him entertained, because I'm not only here to do a job, I'm needed in the burns unit. I can't just walk away from that to show Patrick around.'

She paused, realising something she hadn't considered before.

'Even if I knew where around was! I came from the airport to here, and that's it.'

'I'll show you both around,' Kal said. 'Now the Spanish team is here, it will be easier for you to get away.'

'The Spanish team is surgical,' Nell reminded him. 'They're taking the jobs you and other surgeons were doing, not working on the ward. It could be weeks before things stabilise enough in the unit for anyone to take time off.'

'Everyone needs time off,' Kal argued.

'That's not what I've heard about you,' Nell shot back at him, knowing this argument about work wasn't the issue. Patrick was the issue. She took a deep breath and tackled it.

'I mean it, Kal. You'll have to take time off to be with him. You can't bring him over here then just dump him in my apartment and go back to work. He needs company, and he'll want to see the city and the surrounding country. And don't think you can ask one of your minions to do it and palm off your responsibility that way. No, you brought him over here, it's up to you to look after him.'

But having taken this stand, Nell realised just how dangerous it was. Thrown into his father's company for any length of time, Patrick, at a vulnerable age, couldn't help but be impressed. Nell knew, none better, the magnetic charm Kal could weave so effortlessly. He'd cast a spell and Patrick would be caught in it.

'That's ridiculous, and so's your attitude to work.' Kal's remonstrance interrupted her thoughts. 'You should be seeing the country also. You can work in the mornings and in the afternoons we will all go out.'

All go out?

Like a family?

She erupted into protest.

'Just like that! You're going to organise *my* life now, as well as Patrick's! Well, thanks but, no, thanks. While I'm needed on that ward, I'll stay there.'

'You forget it is my hospital, Nell,' he said, with cold, implacable logic. 'I can forbid you working at all!'

'You'd do that? Put those patients' lives at risk? Just to get your own way? Or is it to pay me back for not telling you about Patrick? Is this spite, Kal? I'd have thought you'd be above that!'

Silence greeted her outburst. A silence that went on for so long she was forced to look up at him.

He looked puzzled, an expression she wouldn't have associated with Kal, and as his eyes searched her face, she felt her antagonism dying away, killed by what seemed like genuine regret in his expression.

'Nell, do we have to argue? Shouldn't we be rejoicing in our son? I— All the way back on the flight all I could think of was seeing you again—seeing you to tell you how grateful I am for the way you've brought him up and how proud I am of that fine boy. But here we are, throwing harsh words at each other. Is there no middle ground where we can meet? No amnesty possible, for the boy's sake if for nothing else?'

Nell stared at him. Of course there should be an amnesty—or something—but if she showed weakness in front of Kal he'd ride straight over the top of her, moving in on her son—on her life—taking over both their lives as if it was his right.

'I'm too tired to talk about this now,' she said, knowing it was a coward's way out, but in part it was true, for exhaustion was weakening her defences and for a moment the thought of having someone take over her life—and the responsibility for Patrick—had seemed exceedingly appealing.

'Food for a starving mother!'

Patrick came through the still open door with a tray of food, but he wasn't alone. A sweet-faced young woman followed him, another tray in her hands.

'I explained I couldn't carry enough for three people— for me and Mum and you, Kal,' Patrick said, putting down his tray then turning to take the second one from the woman, thanking her in English then Arabic. She bobbed her head towards him then departed. 'So the man in charge of the counter down there sent the woman with me.'

He turned towards his father.

'My Arabic must be OK because they seemed to understand me, although they went right off the planet when I said I was your son. Are you a big cheese in this hospital, Kal?'

Nell hid a smile as she looked at the 'big cheese', wondering just how he'd explain his position, both in the hospital and in this country, to Patrick.

'I'm the hospital boss,' he said, and Patrick nodded.

'I thought it must be that,' he said easily, lifting dishes off the trays and setting them in the middle of the dining table. 'Plates, Mum?'

Nell looked around, taking a moment to work out what Patrick was talking about.

'Somewhere in those kitchen cabinets, I guess,' she said, waving her hand towards the cupboards. 'I've only been eating breakfast here and that's sent up from downstairs. All my other meals I've had on the ward.'

Kal knew from his own apartment exactly where the plates would be, and he turned to find them and get cutlery for the three of them, the small task masking his annoyance at himself that Nell had taken on so much virtually since her arrival in this country and he'd done nothing to stop her.

They'd needed her in the burns unit—that was undeniable—but surely he should have seen she was working herself into exhaustion.

He put the plates on the table then took one up in his hand, serving a little from each of the dishes onto it, then placing it in front of Nell.

'Have something to eat then go to bed,' he said, trying hard not to make it sound like an order. 'Your mother's been up all night with a patient,' he explained to Patrick. 'So after we've eaten, I'll take you for a drive around the city so you can get your bearings.'

He hesitated, eyeing Nell, waiting for a comment. But her head was bent above the plate he'd given her, and all her attention seemed to be on scooping food onto her fork.

'Once you get to know your way around, you can do some exploring on your own. I'd like to show you all I can, but there'll be times when I'll be working.'

'That's OK,' Patrick said easily. 'Mum's always encouraged me to do things on my own, though I would like to learn more Arabic. I can get by with speaking it fairly well but I'm not so good at reading and writing it.'

'I'll find someone to teach you,' Kal said, then he hesitated again, worrying about the boy this time, not Nell. 'That's if you really want to be doing lessons when you're supposed to be on holidays.'

'I don't mind that,' Patrick assured him. 'It'd give me something to do while you and Mum work.'

Nell lifted her head and threw Kal a look that would have shrivelled grass, but Kal knew she couldn't argue and drove home that point, saying easily to Patrick, 'Well, if you're sure that's what you want.'

Conversation then turned to the food, Patrick keen to learn what each dish was called so he knew what to order in future.

Was I so self-confident at his age? Nell wondered, then shook her head. Of course she hadn't been. When she'd been Patrick's age she'd been a mess, embarrassed in adult company, squirming in discomfort with boys, and only secure and confident when surrounded by her girl friends.

Patrick's illness had matured him—she knew that—but seeing him with Kal, the two so alike in manner as well as looks, she wondered if confidence was a genetic thing. She couldn't imagine Kal had ever been a tongue-tied adolescent or known a moment's embarrassment in his life.

'So tell me about your medical tests. What do you have done and how often?'

Nell watched as Patrick turned towards his father, calmly outlining his medication and the regular blood tests he had to have.

'They look for low blood cell counts with the blood tests but I have to watch for other things. Do you know it's T-cell ALL? We found the cancer when I hurt my ribs playing soccer and had a chest X-ray. It showed a shadow in the space between the lungs and they found it was an en-larged… What do you call it, Mum?'

'Thymus. That's where the T-cells are made. You had an enlargement there and in the lymph nodes.'

'Thymus, that's it.' He patted his chest. 'It's in here, in some bit they call the media—something, but of course you'd know that. But with T-cell, other lumps and bumps can grow. It's like…'

He stopped again and looked at Nell.

'Lymphoma,' she offered, not interrupting because it pleased her that Patrick had taken the trouble to find out so much about his illness.

'Lymphoma. More like that than leukaemia, in fact. With the first relapse we found a lump in my neck, which was good because it meant we saw it almost straight away. We hadn't been expecting it because the first lot of treatment—you know how they hit you hard with the drugs at first—'

'Remission induction,' Kal put in, and Patrick nodded.

'Then remission consolidation, then maintenance. Well, in the first stage my white cell count dropped very fast, which is usually good news for a cure first time round, but then we found the lump straight after the consolidation and we had to do stage one again. So now I look for lumps and bumps or swellings anywhere and everywhere, including in embarrassing places, as well as having the blood tests every week.'

Kal was frowning and Nell wondered if he was again thinking he should have been there for his son, although personally she'd have given anything not to have had to go through that dreadful time again.

'How did you manage when they found he'd relapsed?' he asked her a little later when Patrick had returned to the canteen for sweets.

'I was thinking about that just then,' she admitted. 'Most people ask how I felt when Patrick was first diagnosed, but there's so much to do, so many specialists to see, all the different drugs and the effects they'll have on his body to learn about and then to explain it all to him. So I was too busy to think of anything but getting him treated and keeping him positive, but the second time…'

She couldn't speak as the remembered horror of that news flooded over her.

'That's why I had to come,' she said at last. 'I had to know there was some hope ahead of us should that dreadful day ever come again.'

Then, without looking at Kal, she stood up, pushing

her chair back with her legs, holding onto the table as if she were eighty years old.

'I need to sleep,' she said, and turned away.

Then Kal was there, his arm around her, supporting her, offering comfort she didn't want to accept.

'I'll take care of him,' Kal said, his voice gruff but not with anger this time.

Nell nodded, though she had no idea whether he was talking about the bone-marrow test or looking after Patrick that afternoon while she slept.

And right now she wasn't sure she cared, until Kal kissed her on the top of her head, then turned her in his arms so she was held in his embrace.

This time the kiss wouldn't be on the top of her head. She knew that but she couldn't move away.

'Sex in the afternoon? *Come on*, guys!'

Patrick's comment spun them apart and though Kal's face was thunderous as he turned towards his son, Nell touched his arm.

'Teenage humour,' she said quietly, though to Patrick she said, 'You watch your mouth, young man!' Then she headed for the bedroom, too tired to be bothered what happened between the two of them.

She woke four hours later. It was dark outside and the silence in the apartment told her she was on her own. She turned on the bedside light and noticed for the first time that someone had been in and unpacked the parcels Yasmeen had brought to the apartment—how long ago?

She rubbed her face with her hands, unable to work out quite how long she'd been here—wondering if perhaps this was jet-lag.

Whatever! She could see toiletries on the dressing-table, and through the partially opened wardrobe doors noticed clothes hanging neatly.

But the light also revealed a note on the bedside table and she picked it up.

'We're in my apartment, thinking in terms of dinner at about eight. If you wake up, come and join us, otherwise make sure you get something sent up for yourself.'

It was signed 'Kal', although she'd have known his strong, upright writing anywhere.

Had he brought it in himself and put it there? Had he wanted to look at her as she slept, as she'd looked at him the other night? Or was that just wishful thinking, prompted by the hope that their love-making might have meant something more to him than sex and a display of his dominance over her?

She laughed at her fantasies and got out of bed. It was seven-thirty and she'd already missed hours of Patrick's company. She had no intention of missing more of it, even if it meant putting up with Kal's company as well. She opened the wardrobe, wondering exactly what Yasmeen might have purchased for her that would fit into the 'going out for dinner' category.

Nell was confident that whatever Yasmeen had chosen wouldn't offend the sensibilities or go against the dress code of the local people, but in her heart she hoped the clothes wouldn't be too sensible. Fool that she was, she'd like to look good in front of Kal.

Look good? What she'd really like would be to wear something that would knock his socks off, which was about as likely as all the burns patients miraculously getting better that day.

She ran her fingers past the dark shirts and neat slacks,

then over long, all-encompassing garments in black and navy, finally coming to a dress in midnight blue. It had sleeves, and looked long enough to cover her down to her ankles, but it seemed to have some shape about it and she knew the colour suited her.

She pulled it out and threw it on the bed, then searched the drawers for underwear that might be more inspiring than the neat cotton bras and panties she'd already unpacked and worn.

Nothing to start a red-blooded male's heart racing, not that any red-blooded male—or one in particular—would be seeing her underwear, but there was one set in black. It would look better under the blue than the white she'd been wearing.

She showered, washed her hair and blow-dried it, pleased that it behaved for once and sat down neatly around her head. She'd had moisturiser and some make-up in her handbag which she'd miraculously managed to keep hold of during the emergency, and for the first time since her arrival in Kal's country, she used eye-liner and mascara—understated but enough to make her eyes look bigger—then added lipstick in an effort to make her face looked less tired.

All done, she slipped on the dress, surprised to find it so light she felt as if she was still naked. A plain garment but not a cheap one! She fingered the fabric—a fine-woven silk, she guessed. But it wasn't until she looked at herself in the mirror that she realised just how special the garment was. She looked beautiful—not an adjective she could ever remember using to describe herself. But something about the colour, or the cut, or the combination of both, made her look tall, slim and elegant, while at the same time the dress shimmied down her body so her curves looked curvier, and going in and out in all the right places as well.

'Wow!' she muttered at her reflection.

'Wow!' Patrick echoed when he opened the door of Kal's apartment a few minutes later. 'New dress, Mum?'

But it wasn't Patrick's reaction she was after and although she answered him, she was watching Kal, feeling as well as seeing his scrutiny, so when his eyes met hers, his hot with desire, Nell felt a surge of triumph, then immediately squashed it.

The last thing she needed was Kal desiring her!

Wasn't it?

CHAPTER SEVEN

SHE was beautiful, and Kal ached to tell her, ached to hold her, but so much had gone wrong between them he couldn't find the words.

Couldn't say them either, in front of Patrick.

The reminder aggravated him and he realised for the first time just how awkward having a teenage boy around could make things.

Should have thought of it earlier when he caught you about to kiss her.

Yes, he should have, but he hadn't and now he wanted to tell Nell she was beautiful, but it wasn't only Patrick inhibiting him. No matter how attractive Nell was or how attracted he, Kal, was to her, in the back of his mind all the time was the fact that she'd cheated him, and the more he saw of Patrick the more he felt how much he'd lost in not seeing his son grow up and the more his anger at Nell grew.

'So, where are we going, Kal? Do you mind me calling you Kal?'

Patrick grinned at him, then added, 'I'm sure you'd like it better than me calling you Pops!'

'Pops?' Kal echoed weakly, then as Patrick fell about laughing he realised it was a joke and smiled. Nell was smiling, too, a small smile, though the glint in her eyes suggested she'd thought it just as funny as Patrick had but didn't want to laugh.

And seeing her, with the smile on her delicately painted lips and the light glimmering in her amazing, cool grey eyes, his body stirred with a desire so deep and strong it startled him.

How could anger and desire co-exist, so both were equally fierce emotions?

'Kal's fine,' he said, then realised he'd spoken too abruptly when Patrick, who'd been heading for the elevator, turned back towards him. 'Really!' Kal added in a gentler tone, reminding himself of the sensitivities of adolescents.

He took Nell's elbow and guided her along the corridor behind Patrick, who was now loping along, bowling an imaginary cricket ball.

'Does he play cricket as well as soccer?' Kal asked Nell, inwardly congratulating himself on his outward composure, given the state of his mind and the problem desire had caused in his body.

'He did,' Nell said. 'He's sports mad, although his one great desire has always been to learn more about falconry.'

She turned towards Kal and smiled—at him, not Patrick this time—causing him more discomfort.

'I should never have told him about your birds.'

'I'll take him to see them, of course,' Kal told her, then realised Patrick had stopped bowling and was waiting for them to catch up.

'To see your falcons? You would? Cool! When?'

Nell laughed.

'There's a certain immediacy at that age,' she told Kal,

who could only look at this beautiful, laughing woman and shake his head.

He considered himself something of an expert where women were concerned. Admittedly, as the hospital had grown and his responsibilities had grown with it, he'd had less time for dalliance, but when he and his wife had divorced, he'd discovered a single man was in great demand, particularly with the ex-pats who lived, worked and played in the burgeoning city. So he'd had no trouble at all finding women with whom to enjoy a pleasant, relaxed, no-strings-attached relationship.

But Nell? He had no idea where he stood with her as far as a relationship was concerned.

Not a clue! Most of the time they'd spent together had been in argument, which had put distance between them, but earlier today, when he'd been about to kiss her, she hadn't moved away.

And that night—he'd lost count of how many nights ago it had been—she'd responded to his love-making with so much ardour she must still feel something for him—even if it was only physical! So how could she be so cool? How could her body not be burning for a repeat session, and how could it not be tied in knots of frustration over the situation with Patrick being there?

The anger bubbled to the surface again. He scowled at her then regretted it as her laughter faded.

'What now?' she demanded quietly, as Patrick stepped into the elevator ahead of them.

Kal shook his head, then offered a smile himself. It would definitely lack the radiance of hers, but right now a partial, forced stretching of the lips was the best he could do.

'So, where are we going?'

Patrick repeated the question he'd asked earlier, and

Kal, relieved to have something other than his libido to think about, answered him.

'There's a restaurant on the top floor of a new building on the seashore. Remember as we came in to land I showed you how the Gulf of Arabia curls into the land?'

'And you said you used to go fishing where all the sky-scrapers are now?' Patrick replied. 'Cool!'

Nell watched her son interacting with his father and felt an ache in the region of her heart. Not only had she denied Kal the opportunity to see his son grow up—a denial she was certain he would never forgive—but she'd denied Patrick a father.

Had she done the wrong thing all those years ago?

'Mum goes off into a fugue state like that now and then,' she heard Patrick say, and wondered what she'd missed of the conversation.

They were exiting the elevator now, not on the ground floor where she'd been before but into a well-lit basement. Kal led the way to a big, black, four-wheel-drive vehicle, and the lights on it flickered as he released the door locks.

'Kids in the back,' he said to Patrick, who accepted the decree with only a token protest, although, as Nell settled into the front passenger seat, she wished she'd had the foresight to grab the back seat for herself. Admittedly the car was wide, but Kal was still too close, the energy his body seemed to radiate buzzing against her skin, while his aftershave—a musky tang she wouldn't have said she liked had she sniffed it in a shop—permeated all her senses, firing her body to an agony of desire she hadn't felt for fourteen years and had never thought to feel again.

'Comfortable?' Kal asked.

'No!' came out before she'd considered the repercussions.

Kal smiled as if he knew exactly why she'd said it, but of course Patrick had to ask.

'It's the dress,' she told him, which both was and wasn't a lie. She was reasonably sure it was the feel of the silk brushing against her body that was making whatever Kal was doing to her worse, but the excuse she offered Patrick had nothing whatsoever to do with the fabric. 'I lost my luggage when I arrived and Yasmeen, a doctor I work with, was kind enough to go out and get me some clothes, which is just as well as I haven't had a spare moment to myself. And though the dress is beautiful, you know me, Patrick, more at home in jeans and a cotton shirt.'

'Or a miniskirt,' Patrick reminded her. 'You've still got great legs, Mum,'

'Tha-ank y-o-u,' Nell said, making her voice sound old and croaky, concentrating on Patrick so she could ignore the questioning look Kal was throwing her way.

'Mum used to wear a miniskirt to cricket matches in summer until all my friends started getting older and whistling.'

Why had she brought up her son to be so open and forthcoming? Why couldn't he be like the teenagers she knew who were content to sit silent and slightly surly in adult company?

'But I guess women don't wear miniskirts much in this country,' Patrick continued, 'though you'd see Mum still had good legs if you took us swimming.'

A ripple of apprehension feathered along Nell's spine. Was Patrick's conversation more than idle chatter?

Surely he couldn't be trying to push them together? And, if so, why?

Nell shook her head at her own stupidity. So he'd have two parents instead of one, of course.

But he had that now.

Kal had made some reply to Patrick's comment but Nell had missed it, and, thankfully Kal was now pointing out landmarks they were passing, probably to her as well as to Patrick, though she wasn't listening. She was working again on sorting out a few priorities in her head. Number one was Patrick's health. She'd have to speak to Kal again about the bone-marrow tests. Number two had always been Patrick's emotional well-being—in fact, until he'd got sick that had been number one.

And as he'd never had an on-the-spot father—he'd been too young to remember much of Garth being around—why should he want one now? Fathers were all well and good, and this father in particular would be very useful for Patrick to have in his teenage and young adult years, but a permanent fixture in *both* their lives? Nell couldn't see that it was necessary at all.

'They call this building the big rig,' Kal was saying when Nell tuned back into the conversation. 'People think at night, when it's lit up as it is, it looks like one of the oil rigs out in the desert. Before oil was discovered, this was such a poor country the symbolism of the rig is very important.'

He paused then he added, 'To some.'

'You don't sound very certain about that,' Nell said to him as they pulled up in a well-lit entry and an attendant appeared to open her door.

'Oh, it's been good for the people in many ways,' Kal told her, remaining in his seat although the door on his side had also been opened. 'The hospital is just one instance. But we're losing so much of the old way of life.

Patrick spoke of miniskirts. Our young girls are not going that far, but it is the loss of values that comes with change. That bothers me.'

He got out, leaving the attendant to park the car, and joined Patrick and Nell on the pavement.

'Values?' Patrick queried, as they were walking through the foyer of the hotel. 'What kind of values, Kal?'

'Family values first and foremost,' Kal told him, and Nell wondered if some of what she'd been thinking might have gone out in thought waves into his head. 'It's the structure of the family that has held my people...' He punched Patrick lightly on the shoulder and amended, 'Our people together. You will have heard tales of the male being the head of the household and as such entitled to respect, well, that is so, but it's the women who have held the tribes together, who know all the family history. They know who's related to who and how, and they teach the young children the importance of loyalty and honour and integrity because these are the things that helped the Bedouin tribes survive the hardships of the desert through thousands of generations. They allow we men to think we have the power, but in truth it is the women who run our lives.'

'Same in our family,' Patrick told him gloomily. 'Gramps and I might have great ideas about weekends away—going off fishing for a few days—but he always has to ask Gran and I always have to ask Mum!'

Kal laughed and put his arm around his son, and Nell, seeing the two heads so close together, felt her heart bump about in her chest. Kal was telling Patrick that wasn't quite what he'd meant, but over his son's head his eyes met hers, and the message in those eyes reignited the deep throb of desire she'd felt earlier.

Forget it. With Patrick there, it was impossible to do

anything about it—which was a *good* thing because seductively delicious sex with Kal would only weaken her defences against a man who was used to getting his own way.

'We go up to the top floor,' Kal was saying, but his eyes continued to tease hers, as if he knew exactly the effect he was having on her.

The elevator took them swiftly upwards and spilled them out into a restaurant that looked out over the city to the south and darkness to the north. A bowing waiter led them to a table by a window, and Patrick, who'd at least seen something of the city that afternoon, now wanted some landmarks pointed out so he could get his bearings.

'Wait!' Kal said, settling opposite Nell and turning to the waiter to order drinks and a platter of finger food on which they could nibble while they decided on their meals.

'Now, see the building with the blue light on the top?' he said to Patrick. 'That's the hospital. This afternoon we drove from there down to the docks so if you look to the right you'll see the lights along the darkness of the Gulf. That's where cruise ships berth and container ships carrying foodstuff and goods. If you look further down there you'll see the lights of the bunkers where the oil tankers take on their loads.'

The waiter returned with a tray of different-coloured drinks.

'So many!' Nell gasped as the man unloaded the tray onto the table.

'Different fruit juices and combinations of juices. I didn't know what you and Patrick might like, so I ordered a selection.'

He smiled—at her, not Patrick—and she felt again the

shimmy of attraction in her skin and the heat of it warming her body.

'This is one you should try. Persimmon juice.'

He passed her the glass, his fingers brushing hers, oh, so casually, yet deliberately, Nell knew.

He was seducing her right in front of their son!

Why?

To prove Patrick would be no barrier to their relationship?

What relationship?

Nell sipped her drink, only half listening to Patrick's chatter as he tried different drinks, giving them marks out of ten for drinkability.

The persimmon juice was both sweet and tart at the same time—not unlike the man who'd offered it—although it had been a long time since he'd been sweet to her.

No, he'd been sweet today when she'd told him of the man's death—

'Did you do anything about an autopsy?' she asked, pleased to have something to take her mind off obsessing over Kal.

'Yuck, Mum! We're out at dinner. No autopsy talk, OK?'

Kal smiled at Patrick's complaint but nodded to Nell.

'It was being done this afternoon. Results will be on my desk in the morning—'

He stopped suddenly and smiled at her.

'Actually, they'll be on my desk by the time we get back to the hospital. And since Patrick is obviously averse to such things, we could drop him back at the apartment then go across and take a look. You haven't seen my office yet, have you?'

Nell couldn't believe this was happening! Oh, the conversation was OK—on the surface it all made perfect sense—but there was no way Kal was talking about autopsy results. He was teasing and tempting her—challenging her, in fact—to be alone with him. He'd been sending seductive vibrations her way since she'd turned up at his apartment door, and now he was upping the ante—offering a way they could do something about the attraction that was simmering between them, without in any way affecting or offending Patrick.

'Here!'

Now he'd lifted a small round ball of food and was offering it to her in his fingers, leaning across the table, his eyes holding hers.

'Try it, Mum, it's delicious. And after that you can try this little pastry thing. What's its name again, Kal?'

Kal replied to Patrick's query but his eyes still held Nell's, daring her not to take the food into her mouth. She opened her lips and his fingertips brushed against them, fanning the flames of desire she was feeling right through her body.

'Great, isn't it? I told Kal not to tell you if any of the things that went into the food were particularly gross, but he said most dishes are made of meat or beans or nuts, not sheep's eyes and things like that.'

'Sheep's eyes?' Nell echoed faintly, nausea easing a little of the desire. 'Tell me I didn't just eat a sheep's eye.'

Patrick laughed, but all Kal said was, 'Would I do a thing like that to you?'

I don't know, Nell wanted to reply. You're doing plenty of other stuff I'd rather you didn't!

But with her body feeling more alive than it had in years, she knew that wasn't entirely true. She didn't want Kal seducing her with his eyes, and his smile, and his tempting fingers, but that was because any kind of relationship between them would complicate things, not because she didn't like what he did to her.

Not only would it complicate things but she'd end up hurt. Losing Kal once had been bad enough—but to lose him twice? No, she couldn't handle that.

But he talked of marriage?

Marriage without love, the hard-headed bit of her brain reminded her. He'd talked of love, too, and not with any affection for it or belief in it!

'She might be asleep, sitting up with her eyes open!'

Patrick's comment made her realise she was missing something.

Missing something? The evening was turning into a nightmare. She was eating food and sipping her drink while her mind argued about love relationships and her body hummed with...

What?

Lust, the hard-head offered, but surely it was more than that.

'I'm sorry,' she said, finally responding to Patrick's continued teasing. 'I must be more tired than I thought. But I'm with you now. What were you talking about?'

'Kal was pointing out more landmarks,' Patrick told her. 'See over there, at the edge of the city lights, there's a big square of lights with a scattering of lights inside it. That's his family's compound. It's kind of like a small suburb because his father and brothers and some other relatives all have their own houses inside it. Kal has a house there, though he uses the apartment at the hospital because it's easier for him to get to work if he's needed urgently.'

Had Kal explained all that while she'd been lost in thought?

Ashamed to have been so inattentive, Nell peered obediently towards the square of lights.

'They have bright lights around the outside of the compound to keep the djinns away. Djinns are spirits—they can be good or bad, but usually they are mischievous more than bad and though these days people don't really believe in djinns, they don't exactly not believe in them either, Kal says.'

Nell glanced towards this oracle her son was quoting.

'I think maybe my man who died had a bad djinn,' she suggested, but looking at Kal wasn't a good idea so she turned back to the window, determined to get with the conversation and put all thoughts of desire and seduction firmly out of her mind.

'Is the compound on the water? Is the blackness beyond it a branch of the Gulf?'

'No, the blackness beyond it is the desert,' Kal said, and something in his voice—the way he said the words—brought desire and seduction right back, not only into her mind but into her body as well.

Not long after they'd met they'd gone to stay on South Stradbroke island, taking a water taxi with a group of friends to camp there for the weekend. The others had teased Kal about the camping, telling him he should be the expert, and expert he was. But late that first night, when their friends had been drinking around the fire, she and he had walked across to the ocean side of the island and sat on the top of a high sand dune, looking out over the water.

It had been a moonless night, and Kal had turned to her.

'It looks like the desert. In the darkness, the soft ridges of the waves could be the dunes,' he'd said quietly. 'It looks like home.'

She'd heard the depths of his homesickness in those

words and had put her arms around him, offering comfort, letting him talk.

'It even sounds the same. When the wind whips the sands across the dunes, you hear that shushing sound the waves are making. I'd love to take you to the desert, Nell. Love to show you all the places that mean so much to me—to have you share them with me. But I can't do that.'

He'd turned to her and kissed her then held her hands and told her of the bargain he'd made with his parents, and how his values meant he had to honour it.

'So, nothing can be between us but friendship, my lovely Nell,' he'd whispered, tangling his hands in her hair and looking deep into her eyes. It had been then that she'd known there would be more, because a little love and joy and rapture shared with Kal would be better than none.

She'd told him so, and that night, in the dunes, with the ocean making desert noises beside them, they'd made love for the first time.

Turning back from the window, she glanced at him, and knew he'd been thinking of that time as well. Just so had their thoughts always matched, but back then there'd been love to bind them together—a love that had been deeper and stronger and more desperately passionate because they had known it wouldn't be for ever.

CHAPTER EIGHT

OR SO she'd thought. Maybe she'd just imagined he'd felt as she had. No matter what had happened back then, here and now was a different matter. Here and now he only wanted marriage because he wanted Patrick, and he was using the undeniable attraction he knew still existed between them to tempt her into it.

'So what are we going to eat?'

She asked the question of Patrick who'd been perusing the menu, comparing the English side of it to the Arabic and pointing out to his father the words he knew.

Patrick rattled off a list of incomprehensible dishes, assuring Nell she'd enjoy all of them, then he looked at Kal.

'Is that all right? It won't cost too much, will it? Mum always likes to pay our share, but she took leave to come over here to show the skin spray, so I wouldn't like her to use up all her holiday money on one dinner.'

'I will pay for dinner,' Kal said, in a voice that forbade any further discussion on the matter, and this time the look he turned on Nell was the angry one again—all hint of seduction or remembered love-making burnt away.

Fortunately Patrick, with the insouciance of youth, failed

to notice the change in the atmosphere at the table and chattered blithely throughout the meal, questioning Kal about the dishes, about the city and about the way his people lived.

Nell found the food delicious but she couldn't enjoy it as she should have, aware the whole time of the difference in the man across the table, puzzling over how such an innocuous remark of Patrick's could have turned him back into the arrogant Kal.

She was thankful when the meal was finally over and they left the building, but although she tried to slip in front of Patrick into the back seat, telling him he'd see the landmarks he now knew better from the front, it was not to be.

'No way, Mum, you sit up front with Kal. I'll sit back here and pretend we're a family. Mum, Dad and the kid in the back. Glad I've got beyond kiddie seats.'

Patrick was just rattling on, Nell told herself, but one glance at Kal's grim profile told her the words had done more than rattle *him*—they'd made him even more angry than he'd been earlier. In fact, if she hadn't known better she'd have been sure he was muttering expletives under his breath.

Though maybe, not being used to adolescent company, he was praying for patience.

He pulled into his parking space in the basement car park. Patrick got out and opened Nell's door, waiting for her to get out then giving her a hug.

'I'm having the best time,' he whispered to her, and Nell felt guilt swamp her again, this time for being so ungracious about the attention Kal was paying the boy.

'That's great,' she said to Patrick, wanting to add, Make the most of it. But he'd ask why and things might get very sticky.

'So, Patrick, have you checked out the channels we get on TV? There are two local channels in Arabic and all the rest are cable, so you get mostly US or UK programmes.' Kal asked the question as they went up in the elevator.

Patrick assured Kal he'd got it figured, then yawned.

'But I don't think I'll be watching much TV tonight. If feeling like you've been run over by a bus is jet-lag, I've got it.'

'Run over by a bus?' Nell went into immediate panic mode. 'Were your last tests OK? When were they? Have you missed one? Any lumps?'

Patrick put his hands on her shoulders.

'Relax, Mother-worrier. I'm just tired from the flight. I know I slept this morning, but that couldn't have been enough.'

He leaned forward and kissed her on the cheek, then gave her a quick hug, while Kal, his face unreadable, held the elevator doors open, waiting for the exchange to finish and the pair of them to exit.

They walked up to the apartment together but as Nell made to follow Patrick through the door, Kal held her back.

'You're forgetting the autopsy result will be in my office.'

Nell looked at him, but the desire that had tempted her earlier was gone from his face, replaced by an unreadable mask.

'I'm tired, too. I'll read it in the morning.'

'By morning it will be filed away and if, as you believe, that consultant had something to do with your patient's death, you'll never know.'

He was not quite blackmailing her but definitely daring her to accompany him to his office. Why?

She glanced towards Patrick who, although he'd pleaded tiredness, was using the remote to flick through the television channels.

'Go and read the horrible thing,' he said to her, without taking his eyes off the screen. 'I've already unpacked in the second bedroom and if I can't find anything to watch for a while on TV, I'll go to bed and read.'

But Nell still hesitated.

'Scared, Nell?' Kal whispered, so only she could hear, and although she knew it was a goad to make her do something she didn't want to do, she fell for it, determined he wouldn't guess just how confused she was.

'Of you? As if!'

She turned back to Patrick and blew him a goodnight kiss.

'That's in case you're asleep by the time I come back. If you're still sleeping in the morning, I'll leave a number where you can call me when you wake up.'

'Oh, don't worry about the morning. Kal and I are leaving early to go out to the desert,' Patrick said cheerfully.

'Oh! Well, have fun!' Nell managed to say, although her throat was tight with anger. She shut the door and faced the man who, not content with seducing her with his eyes across the table, was now seducing her son away from her.

'And just when was this little expedition arranged?' she demanded, so furious with Kal that once again she wanted to beat her fists against his chest. Only last time she'd tried that he'd captured her and his touch had done weird things to her anger...

'This afternoon. Patrick did mention it at dinner but you might not have been listening.'

'And how long is this desert jaunt going to last? Will

he miss his blood tests? Will you make sure he takes his tablets?'

Kal put his hands on her shoulders and looked down into her face.

'Do you think I wouldn't make sure he took his tablets? Could you believe I am so insensitive I could find my son only to lose him to a disease? Can you think so badly of me, Nell?'

Nell tried to move away but his grip tightened.

'I don't know what to think of you!' she snapped. 'Your arrogance, your attitude, your changing moods, I don't understand any of it. Like tonight—come and see the autopsy report now or forget it! That's close to blackmail, Kal. Why? Why couldn't a copy have been left for me in the office on the ward? Why push me like you did to come now?'

'You don't know?' he asked, his eyes blazing into hers, not with the desire she'd seen earlier, but with something she didn't understand.

Something that made her feel uncertain—not afraid exactly, but certainly wary.

'No, I don't know!' He'd relaxed his grip and she managed to slip away. 'But now I'm here, let's get it done.'

She walked away, back the way she usually went to cross the pedestrian walkway to the hospital, assuming his office was somewhere that way.

His long strides soon overtook her quick angry ones, but he didn't stop her, neither did he speak. He simply walked along beside her back to the elevator, pressed numbers into a keypad to take it up, then guided her out and along another corridor.

Eventually he stopped at a door, pulled out his keys,

unlocked the door and held it for her to go inside. She entered what must have been an anteroom to his office, set up, she imagined, so he could hold small staff meetings in comfort, because over by the windows there was a long couch and several armchairs grouped around a coffee-table, while closer to an inner door was a desk with all the usual paraphernalia of a secretary or personal assistant.

He herded her into the anteroom then pointed to an armchair.

'Sit!' he commanded.

Nell moved towards the chair, but turned back before she lowered herself into it.

'Should I beg as well?'

Kal looked at her for a moment, then the mask cracked and a smile that sent shivers down her spine lit up his face.

'Later,' he said, silky smooth! 'Much later. For now, we need to talk. Do you want a tea or coffee? An alcoholic drink perhaps? I keep some for visitors.'

Nell shook her head. She was twitchy enough about what was going on here—alcohol would surely make her even more uptight.

Apparently satisfied he'd done his duty as a host, Kal took the chair opposite her, then leaned forward so he was barely two feet away, not quite invading her personal space but close enough to make the twitchiness worse.

'Do you deliberately set out to make me angry, Nell? Is it some kind of punishment because I left Australia? Because you were pregnant?'

He paused as if waiting for a reply, but Nell couldn't make sense of the questions, let alone fashion a reply.

'When have I made you angry?'

With that question, apparently, from the frown on his face!

Kal caught himself before he exploded and contented himself with a glare at the infuriating woman who had turned his life upside down.

'You do it all the time,' he told her, letting a little of his fury bubble in the words. 'You've come over here on *leave*—that's what Patrick said. You're not even being paid! Do you think that doesn't make me feel terrible?'

'But Patrick told you that, not me,' Nell protested. 'And I took leave to come over because part of why I was coming was personal—in fact, to me, the biggest part was personal—so it was hardly fair to expect to get paid.'

Kal couldn't believe anyone could be so naïve. He stood up to stop himself from reaching out to shake her and strode across the room to relieve some stress.

'Everyone in the universe does personal things on their fully paid-for, work-related jaunts. You must know that. You must have been to conferences where half the attendees are out playing golf when they should be attending lectures and the other half are usually getting over hangovers.'

'I don't go to many conferences,' Nell said quietly, and realising she probably didn't go because of Patrick made Kal even angrier.

'This is what I mean. That boy thought you should pay for half the meal, and he was worrying about what it would cost you. It was my responsibility to see you and he never wanted for anything—that you never had to worry about money. How do you think I feel that you've taken that away from me and struggled to juggle work and bringing up *my* son?'

She looked at him, her eyes wide, her expression puzzled.

'Kal, it was my decision to go through with the pregnancy, and that made Patrick my responsibility. I've never regretted it and, yes, at times it's been tough, but he's never wanted for anything vital and at the same time he's not been spoilt. He knows the value of money and that he can't have everything he wants just because he wants it. If it's something I won't buy, he has to save for it. Would you throwing money at us have made a difference to how I brought him up? I don't think so!'

Good, she'd stopped looking puzzled and was angry now, but not as angry as he was, although he couldn't pin his anger down to one single point.

'That still doesn't alter the fact you're not being paid—you're working at my hospital for nothing.'

'I'm a doctor, it's what I do, but if it's going to make you feel better and stop this ridiculous conversation, then pay me. Put me on the payroll and pay me whatever you pay Yasmeen. Now, shall we look at the autopsy report?'

'Do you really believe I brought you here for that reason? If the report is on my desk, there'll be a copy of it on your desk, too. It will be marked private and for your eyes only, although you can discuss it with Yasmeen as the senior local doctor in the ward.'

'Well, in that case, I'll be off,' Nell announced, ignoring his question and standing up, her departure, as far as he could see, imminent.

'Nell?'

She looked at him and sank back down into the chair.

'OK,' she said. Faint colour was rising in her cheeks but she held his eyes with a defiance he had to admire.

'When you first talked about coming here to see the autopsy report, I thought it was a ploy for the two of us to be together, and I'd be a liar if I didn't admit that the physical attraction between us is still strong, and the thought of us being able to do something about it was very appealing. But during dinner I was thinking about where our relationship began—thinking about love, Kal. I think you loved me then—I certainly loved you—but I've made the mistake of going into a relationship without love once before and I'm not going to do it again, no matter how enjoyable the sex might be.'

'Love! You talk of love? What is it, Nell? Quantify it or define it for me. Oh, I fancied I was in love back then, but if what I felt for you was love, then let me tell you it's an emotion I never wish to experience again. Not for what it was at the time, but for the fallout, which proved more deadly than nuclear waste. Shall I tell you what love did for me, Nell?'

She didn't answer but he told her anyway. Told her of the sweet young bride who'd cried into her pillow night after night, unable to conceive because of her unhappiness and made more unhappy by that inability.

'I was kind to her, and gentle, and tried everything I could to make her happy, Nell, but some part of me was locked away from her. She knew that instinctively, and though she never probed, she felt lessened by it and in the end she returned to her father's house, causing pain in both our families, shame in mine. Now she studies and hopes to teach eventually at the university. Philosophy, Nell! Does it encompass love?'

So bitter, Nell thought sadly, but she wasn't going to let him get away with that.

'Everything encompasses love, or it should,' she told him, tilting her chin so he'd know she had no intention of giving in on this point. 'Love isn't just something between people—it's a warm feeling inside you. Maybe if your ex-wife enjoys learning and teaching, she'll find the warmth and comfort of love in her job. Maybe the marriage wasn't any more right for her than it was for you. But don't knock my belief in love, Kal, don't even try. Love has given me the best memories of my life and a beloved son. How could I not believe in it?'

She stood up again and walked towards the door, and this time he didn't try to stop her. Neither did he say anything, which was just as well because Nell's heart was pounding so rapidly she doubted she could have answered. Opening the door, she was tempted to look back at him, but looking at Kal was a dangerous occupation so she continued right on out.

'We'll still get married!'

The words echoed down the corridor and she spun back towards him, forgetting she didn't want to look at him.

He was standing in the doorway, leaning against the jamb, a look of implacable determination on his face.

'You've *got* to be joking!' she snapped.

'Not for one minute,' he said. 'Patrick's my son, you will be my wife!'

'Just what century are you living in, Kal?' Nell demanded, coming back towards him so he couldn't fail to see how serious she was. '"You will be my wife," indeed? What will you do next? Fling me over a camel and ride off with me into the desert?'

'No, but I'll fight you for my son. I'll fight you in any court in any land, and I'll prove I can give him a better life. More than that, he's nearly fourteen. The judge will ask his opinion. And you've given me the task of looking after him while you work. Do you think he will want to go back to a tame life in Australia when he sees what I can offer?'

Pain so great she wondered if she was having a heart attack squeezed Nell's chest and she reached out to the wall for support.

'You'd do that? You'd do that to me?' The words sounded like a pitiful mew, even to her own ears, but Kal wasn't moved. If anything, he looked more fiercely unyielding.

'You've kept him from me for all these years,' he reminded her in the cold, remote voice she found so unsettling. 'Yes, I'd do it.'

Nell turned and walked away. She'd have liked to have kept a hand on the corridor wall for support but she was damned if she was going to let him see—again—just how devastated she was. She reached the elevators and leant against the wall for a moment, wondering what to do next, too upset to think straight.

She couldn't go back to the apartment—if Patrick was still up, he'd guess she was upset. There'd be coffee in the canteen, although she wasn't certain it operated twenty-four hours a day, and coffee might make her more uptight.

The ward! She needed to see the autopsy report some time. She'd go down to the ward, sit quietly in the doctor's office and read it.

Or pretend to read it while she sorted out her head.

All was quiet on the ward, although several of the patients, as she went from bed to bed, unable to be there without checking on them, were awake, their injuries making sleep difficult.

She picked out the three new post-op patients because the limbs that had received skin grafts were splinted and swathed in bandages to prevent movement. The young girl with the facial wounds was sleeping, but a woman all but covered in the now-familiar black veils sat by her side, the rubber gloves and medical face mask she wore looking out of place with her traditional dress.

Nell smiled at her, and the woman's eyes smiled back above the mask.

'Her skin is healing,' Nell said quietly, peering at the girl's cheek. The woman nodded, then touched the girl lightly on the arm.

'Her heart will take longer,' she said, her English clear and understandable. 'I am her aunt, but an aunt can't replace a mother and a father, though I will try.'

Nell felt tears well in her eyes and though she knew they were probably to do with her own emotional trauma, she touched the woman on the arm.

'I am sure you will do a wonderful job,' she whispered, then she left the ward, afraid that if she encountered any more emotionally fraught situations she'd end up crying like a baby.

The autopsy report—had Kal had it translated into English for her?—was on her desk, and she slumped into the chair and looked at it, not really reading the words.

Until she came to 'gross internal bleeding' and had to start at the beginning again. The heart consultant had inserted the catheter into the man's femoral artery and through it to the left ventricle, where he'd closed a slight hole in the ventricular septum. But somewhere along the line, maybe as he'd withdrawn the instrument on the end of the catheter, he'd nicked the wall of the artery, so small a hole it had gone unnoticed both by him and the radiographer.

Blood had begun to seep from the artery, then, as less blood had reached the man's leg and his brain had told the heart to pump harder, more blood had escaped, enlarging the hole until the volume of it in the chest cavity had constricted the lungs until it virtually squeezed the heart to death.

Accidents happened in medicine, Nell reminded herself, but that didn't stop her anger building at the consultant who'd been so pleased with himself. Not that anything would happen to him. With no relations to fight for his rights, the patient's death would be recorded, the autopsy report filed, and that would be that.

Unless *she* sued on his behalf!

And bring trouble on the hospital? Yasmeen would be involved. Did the friendship she'd offered Nell deserve to be repaid that way?

Kal, too?

Was she thinking of this as some kind of payback to Kal?

Nell shook her head. She didn't have a vindictive bone in her body—though she did feel anger towards the consultant.

But realistically she didn't know much about medicolegal law in her own country, let alone in this one, so how would she go about getting justice for her patient?

And what would it achieve?

She was pondering all these questions and getting absolutely nowhere when the door of the office opened and Kal appeared.

'I thought I might find you here,' he said, waving what was apparently his copy of the autopsy report towards her. 'I'll need legal opinion, of course, but the consultant is definitely responsible. I'll suspend him from working in this hospital immediately and find out what other course we should take against him. The patient not having a family makes it difficult, but his death shouldn't just be pushed aside as an unfortunate accident.'

'But if you take legal action, the hospital will also be included in the responsibility for the man's death,' she reminded him.

'So?'

Nell stared at him, unable to believe what she was hearing. This was the Kal she'd once known, the man to whom truth and honour had been so important—important enough to be pursued even at the risk of hurting the hospital. So maybe it was truth that had made him hurt her by denying love. Maybe he really did believe the emotion she called love was nothing but a destructive force.

'Are you listening to me?' he demanded, and she shook her head.

'Not really,' she admitted. 'I got lost after you said we shouldn't push his death aside as an unfortunate accident. I was thinking the same thing when you came in, but didn't know what to do about it, or even if there was anything we could do.'

'I'll do something,' he promised, then his gaze moved over her, and for the first time since things had fallen apart in the restaurant his face softened.

'You spent your first few days here telling me to go to bed. I'm telling you that now, Nell. You look exhausted.'

He paused, then allowed a rueful smile to flick across his lips.

'Beautiful, but exhausted.'

He held out his hand towards her.

'Come, I'll take you up to the apartment. Your apartment, not mine, though that discussion isn't finished!'

Nell took his hand and let him pull her to her feet, then found herself glad of his supporting arm as they made their way back to the apartments. Emotional as well as physical exhaustion was dogging her footsteps now.

And weakening her resolve…

Having someone to lean on, literally as well as figuratively, was a very seductive thought…

CHAPTER NINE

KAL glanced at the boy who sat by his side, looking out of the window, asking questions about the buildings they were passing. He tried to see something of Nell in the profile or in the face when Patrick turned towards him, but all he saw was his own young self.

Then the city slipped away behind them and the long straight road stretched out into the desert.

'Wow! It really is desert,' Patrick said, and Kal smiled.

'Wait until we turn off this road—you won't believe civilisation can be so close.'

He drove swiftly, Patrick talking and asking questions, constantly surprising Kal with his perception and intelligence, then the small marker came in sight and Kal pointed it out.

'Can you make out tyre tracks running away from the main road?' he asked Patrick, who peered obediently through the window.

'Only just,' he said. 'In fact, they seem so faint I might be imagining them.'

'It's because the sand shifts all the time,' Kal told him. 'Desert sands are like the sea, always on the move. We'll get out.'

They walked around to the front of the car where he showed Patrick how to feel for the hardness of a much-used track beneath the soft top layer of sand, then pointed out how the 'road' ahead could be seen as slight indentations in the sand.

'But that's for those who don't know the desert,' he explained when they were back in the car. 'Those of us who have lived here know always where we are. Do you know how to find compass points from the sun?'

'I've a vague idea—something about pointing your watch towards the sun? But my watch is digital, so that wouldn't work.'

Kal stopped the car again and, using his watch, showed Patrick how to do it.

'So, in this desert,' he added, when they were driving again, 'all you need to do is to remember the main road runs directly east-west, and we went south off it, so as long as you keep driving north, you'll hit it again somewhere.'

It was basic desert lore and the first of many things he taught his son, although later, when Patrick asked what he'd do to find the north at night, Kal laughed and showed him the compass in the front of the car.

'And this is a GPS—a global positioning system— which gives you the co-ordinates of where you are at all times. It has some locations set into it. See, go to menu— you've got town, oasis, beach and camp. We're going to camp so choose that one.'

Kal drove on while Patrick worked out how to follow the GPS direction, and shouted with delight when they came to where a black tent had been erected.

'The camp?'

'It is,' Kal assured him, feeling so much pleasure and delight in his son's company it was almost painful.

But not as painful as his head, which was throbbing with unrelenting persistence. He knew it was from lack of sleep. He'd spent the night in his office, dictating letters and messages for his secretary, leaving notes for the various unit managers at the hospital and more lengthy notes for the legal people.

Fortunately his men had set up the tent and the cook had prepared food and put it in the refrigerator in the car, so all Kal would have to do was forage in it for lunch and light a fire to cook the meat for the main meal this evening. Not camping out the way Patrick might have expected, but Kal had wanted to spend as much time as he could with the boy.

He walked into the dark coolness of the tent and saw the carpets spread across the floor and a pile of white clothes in a corner.

Patrick had followed him in and was looking around, marvelling at carpets spread on sand.

'Out here, I shed my western clothes,' Kal said to him. 'Will it bother you if I put on a kandora—the long dress—and suffra—our headdress?'

'Great. Can I wear one, too? Or do I have to be a full sheik or something special like you are to get to wear one?'

Kal laughed and went to the pile of clothes.

'You could wear the kandora and, if you like, a coloured suffra—red and white, or black and white check—but I have only white here because that's what I wear. So let's see you as a sheik.'

It was the start of a busy but exhausting day, Patrick wanting to know so much about how Kal's people had lived before oil had changed their lives, wanting to learn to drive, then tearing up and down the sand hills in the big, safe, automatic vehicle, wanting to cook the dinner over an open fire, assuring Kal he was a barbecue expert.

And Kal let him cook, for the headache, which had persisted all day, was now joined by some kind of fever, and though he hid the tremors he was feeling from the boy, he knew they should drive back to town.

Maybe after dinner, although he knew Patrick would be disappointed…

Patrick carried the plate of meat and vegetables he'd cooked on the heavy grill over the fire towards the carpet Kal had spread in front of the tent. Kal had explained that this would be where they ate—cross-legged on the carpet, using their fingers instead of cutlery, an initiation into the Bedouin way. But though Kal was there, he was lying down, and when Patrick spoke to him, he didn't answer.

'Kal!'

Frantic, Patrick shook his father's shoulder, then common sense returned and with it the basic teachings of first aid he'd learned at school. He pressed his fingers against the vein in his father's jaw—and almost cried with relief to feel the throb of a pulse. Kal's chest was rising and falling, too, so he was breathing.

Patrick left him there and ran to the car, remembering the easy steps of starting it, then putting it into gear. He drove it towards his father, praying he wouldn't do something stupid and run over him.

Then, with the back door open, he heaved the man's heavy body up, surprising himself with his own strength, his heart pounding with exertion and fear, a little 'Please, don't die' prayer fluttering continuously on his lips.

Somehow he got Kal in. He looked at the fire and kicked some sand on it, though he doubted it could set light to anything out here, then he ran back to the car and turned it, praying again—this time that he was heading in the right direction to meet the main road back to town.

As he crested the first sand hill he saw a glow on the horizon. Relief flooded through him. All he had to do was drive towards those lights, for that was surely the city.

He hit the main road twenty minutes later. From time to time Kal had mumbled something, but he'd not responded when Patrick had spoken to him so, determined to save his father, Patrick drove on.

The city drew closer and, aware he wasn't very good at steering yet and knowing he'd never handle the big vehicle in traffic, he began to work on a contingency plan. At the first of the big roundabouts on the approach to the city he stopped the car on the verge, turned on the hazard lights and got out, taking off the white robe he'd been wearing so he could wave it to attract attention.

A huge semi-trailer pulled up in front of him, and the driver ran back towards Patrick. He spoke far too quickly for Patrick to understand him, so he grabbed the man's arm and led him to the car, pointing to where his father lay, his breathing now so loud and raspy Patrick was terrified Kal might be dying.

Fortunately the man seemed to understand for he hurried back to his truck then returned a few minutes later, saying the English word 'ambulance' over and over so Patrick would understand.

And an ambulance it was, siren blaring, lights flashing, pulling up beside the truck within very few minutes, paramedics tumbling out.

'It's my father,' Patrick said, relief making his voice tremble and building a huge lump in his throat.

But the men had obviously recognised Kal as an al Kalada, for the name was whispered reverently and the attention became even more urgent.

'Come,' one of the attendants said to Patrick as Kal was loaded into the back of the ambulance. 'Come with us.'

Abandoning the car, Patrick climbed in, only too pleased to have other people in charge—*and* doing the driving. Besides, the ambulance would take Kal to the hospital and Mum was at the hospital. Everything would be all right.

Not wanting to go back to an empty apartment, Nell had stayed on in the burns unit office, checking on test results of all the patients, changing dietary orders where needed, working out which patients might be able to take food by mouth. The office had a wide window in one wall, and some change in the flow of staff traffic past the window made her look up. Staff were gathering in small groups and clusters, talking excitedly and waving their hands.

'What's going on?' she asked when a young ward aide came in with some supper for her.

The girl started to explain in Arabic, then stifled her words with her hands, thought for a few minutes then spoke slowly, as if translating every word she needed into the English she would have learned as a second language at school.

'The sheik, he sick in desert. A boy drive him to town, now ambulance bring him here.'

In this hospital there was only one sheik.

But Kal sick and a boy drove him to town?

Patrick?

But Patrick couldn't drive!

'Where are they now? Where's the boy? What's wrong with Kal—the sheik? What kind of sick?'

The young girl shrugged, Nell's barrage of questions obviously beyond her limited English.

Nell got up, determined to find someone who would understand, but no one she spoke to knew any more than she'd already heard.

Ambulances took people straight to A and E, she reminded herself, and with only a few wrong turns she made her way back to where she'd spent so many hours on the night of her arrival.

Patrick was sitting on a bench by the wall, looking so lost and alone she thought her heart would break.

'Oh, Mum!' he cried as she came towards him, then he stood up and put his arms around her, holding her close while his whole body shook with the release of tension. 'I tried to get someone to phone you, but they didn't seem to understand your name or didn't know what apartment you were in, and I couldn't leave Kal here on his own and go and find you.'

He broke off with the choke of a sob, and Nell held his long, thin body against her own while anger that Kal would put him in this situation gathered in her belly.

Although Kal hadn't done it deliberately.

He was sick?

She patted Patrick's shoulder and held him a little away from her.

'What kind of sick is Kal? What happened, Patrick?'

Patrick's lips began to tremble, as if remembering brought on a panic he hadn't been able to exhibit earlier when Kal's life might have depended on him staying calm.

'He just collapsed, Mum. He'd said earlier he had a headache and I asked why he didn't take something for it, and he said he'd rather wait and see if the desert air cleared it. He said the city often gave him a headache. Then I said I'd do the barbecue and when I brought the meat across he was lying there.'

'And you drove him back—how?' Nell demanded, although her heart was full of fear for Kal. A sudden collapse—a stroke? A brain tumour? Possible diagnoses raced through her mind, but Patrick needed her now—needed to talk through the trauma he'd experienced.

He was explaining how Kal had taught him to drive that morning, and how he'd practised on the sand hills.

Nell hugged him again, praising his courage and his good sense in getting help as soon as he'd got close to the city. Then, as she released him, she saw a group of people sweep through the doors into the ER. A tall, imperious-looking man in a white robe led the way, a small, veiled woman clinging tightly to his arm. Behind this pair were other white robed figures and a gaggle of black-robed women, their faces masked behind the fine veils that fluttered around their heads.

Hospital staff appeared from nowhere, greeting the new arrivals with reverent salaams.

'Let's go, Mum,' Patrick said, and Nell heard panic in the simple words.

She put her arm around his shoulders and led him back the way she'd come in, so he didn't have to pass these people, who were obviously members of Kal's family.

'They will want to see you some time,' she said carefully. 'If only to thank you.'

'Maybe, Mum,' Patrick said, the break in his voice

showing the strain he'd been under. 'But I've just got used to having a father—I don't think I'm ready for more relations. And Kal might not have told them about me. He told me he's not married any more, and hasn't any other children, but whether…'

Nell knew exactly what the 'whether' was—Kal had mentioned introducing Patrick to his family but Nell doubted it would happen any time soon…

Although if they were to get married…

We're not, she reminded herself as they made their way back to the apartment.

'What could be wrong with him?' the boy asked, as the elevator rose towards their floor.

'I don't know, but he's in the best place and in good hands.'

'But you'll find out how he is, won't you, Mum? You'll find someone to ask?'

Nell promised she would, but once inside the apartment she realised Patrick hadn't eaten so she phoned down to order food, then for the first time it struck her that all her son was wearing was a pair of shorts.

'I'd been wearing a kandora—the white gown thing they wear,' he explained. 'But I took it off to wave it at the cars. Must have left it by the road. It's one of Kal's. I hope he won't be angry.'

'I'm sure he won't,' Nell soothed. 'But maybe while we wait for dinner, you could have a shower and get into your pyjamas. You've had a big day, one way and another.'

So Patrick was in the shower when the knock came on the door. Nell opened it, thinking it was their meal, to find the tall man in the white robe she'd seen earlier in ER.

He had a string of amber worry beads in one hand and

she heard the clicking noise they made as he moved them through his fingers. Apart from that, she could only stand and stare, sure this was Kal's father—an important man, a ruler—unsure what he wanted of her.

'I thought you would like to know Khalil has regained consciousness. It seems he has a recurrence of a fever not unlike malaria which he picked up in Africa some years ago. But thanks to the boy's prompt action he was able to be treated swiftly, and though he is very weak and will be kept in hospital for a few days, he will recover.'

Relief from a terror she hadn't fully realised she'd been feeling flooded through Nell.

'Thank you for coming. For telling me,' she said, uncertain whether to ask the man in or not—uncertain what he knew and didn't know.

But the man didn't seem discomfited by her silence. He stood there, clicking through the beads, staring at a point somewhere behind her, his eyes thoughtful. Then finally his gaze turned back to her.

'He is Khalil's son, this boy?'

Oh, hell! Did Kal want his family to know?

Did it matter what he wanted?

Yes, it did, but so did Patrick's birthright.

Nell nodded and the man nodded back at her.

'He told me he had things to discuss and that he would do it soon. I knew of you, of course, from long ago, but not that there was a child.'

There was no reproach in this gently spoken statement, and the lack of it made Nell feel weepy. She swallowed hard, and did her best to explain.

'Kal didn't know either,' she said. 'I knew he was to marry—it seemed unfair to tell him and spoil something that had been arranged and to which he was committed. I knew how much his marriage meant to his family—and how much his family meant to him—so how could I tell him and cause a rift between them?'

'You chose a hard road, but for the boy to have done what he did today, you have raised him well.'

Nell shrugged, not sure she could take too much more of this extraordinary conversation. At that moment Patrick erupted out of the hallway, asking her if she had a spare toothbrush as his was in his bag back in the desert. He stopped when he saw her visitor, hesitated for a moment, then came more quietly towards her.

'Have you heard how Kal is?' he asked, nodding to the visitor but directing the question at his mother.

'He's regained consciousness,' Nell told him, 'and is getting all the treatment he needs. Apparently it was a sudden recurrence of a disease he picked up in Africa some years ago.'

She was aware she was repeating, parrot fashion, what her visitor had said, but although she guessed the man was Kal's father he hadn't introduced himself so she couldn't introduce him to Patrick.

Fortunately he took the matter out of her hands, bowing low to Patrick and touching his hand to his forehead.

'I am your grandfather,' he said in his precise English. 'I am sorry it has taken us so long to meet.'

Patrick, much to Nell's surprise, bowed back, but lower, as if aware of some distinction in obeisance.

'I am Patrick,' her suddenly mature son said. 'I am honoured to meet you, sir.'

And with that he came forward, his hands together, and the other man grasped his shoulders and drew him close, touching his nose to Patrick's nose in what Nell knew was a traditional greeting between male relatives and close friends.

'You did well to get Khalil back to the hospital. Do you drive so young in Australia?'

Patrick grinned at this new relation.

'No, but Kal gave me some lessons this morning and the car's an automatic—it could have driven itself. I'd have been lost without the lights of the city, though. Kal had shown me the GPS but I didn't really know how to work it.'

'You did well,' the man repeated, his voice deeply sincere. Then he turned back to Nell.

'I thank you for the gift of this boy. I will return in the morning.'

And with that he walked away, his back ramrod straight, everything about his bearing betraying his rank.

'Wow!'

Patrick put Nell's reaction into words, but as she was about to close the door she saw a member of staff coming down the corridor, wheeling a trolley she knew would hold their meal.

Patrick was still asleep when Nell was ready to leave for the ward the next morning, but his overnight bag had been delivered and was just inside the door of the apartment. She checked inside to make sure his tablets were there and left him a note, reminding him to take them and giving him the phone number where she could be reached.

'Phone me when you wake up,' she added as a PS on the note, then she took it into his bedroom and left it on the floor just outside his door, where he couldn't fail to see it when he came out. She stood and looked at him for a moment, his gangly, adolescent frame flung with such abandon across the bed.

Weird that she'd come here to get Kal to help Patrick should help be needed, yet it had been Patrick who'd helped Kal.

This would strengthen the bond between them, she knew, and as she left the apartment and saw Kal's father coming towards her, she felt a quailing in her heart. Another bond—another person tying Patrick to this country...

'You are well?' the sheik enquired politely.

'I am well,' Nell responded, 'but Patrick is still sleeping.'

'I have spoken with Khalil this morning and know of Patrick's illness. He will be tired after the excitement of yesterday. With your permission, I will sit in your apartment until he wakes up. Khalil tells me you are needed in the hospital and the boy is his responsibility. I will take that on. He will be safe with me. You need have no fear.'

Nell had no fear—neither did she have a clue how to respond. All she could manage was a feeble 'That's very kind of you', then she rallied and added, 'But there's no need for you to put yourself out. Patrick is used to taking care of himself.'

'Khalil tells me the boy wishes to learn to read and write in Arabic—it will be good for me to be a teacher. You have no objection if we drive? He will learn to read more quickly if he sees road signs and billboards with words he recognises.'

Khalil says—Khalil tells me! It was Patrick all over again. Nell agreed it would be all right and excused herself with the explanation of being needed on the ward, but what she really wanted to do was find out where Khalil al Kalada was and rip his head off. He knew she didn't want this arrangement between him and Patrick to be anything other than a 'getting to know your father' one—not that she'd wanted that!—but even from a hospital bed Kal was weaving a web that was entangling Patrick and drawing him closer and closer into his family.

Patrick should know this other family, conscience reminded Nell, but she was too mixed up to listen to that namby-pamby voice.

Though she'd have to leave ripping off Kal's head until later. She'd left the unit office last night before finishing the jobs that needed doing and would have to get them done now. She also needed to liaise with the Spanish team and make sure the post-op treatment they wanted for their patients was taking place.

Down in the ward, Yasmeen greeted her with the news that Khalil was deathly ill in this very hospital, and Nell nodded, hoping he wasn't really deathly ill while she was feeling so uncharitable towards him. But knowing Yasmeen's opinion of Kal was close to god-like, she decided her friend was probably exaggerating, though as she worked through the morning she was aware of a nagging concern for the man nibbling away at her anger and her determination not to have anything more to do with him.

So at six, after a phone call from Patrick—the fourth of the day, each reporting on where he was and what he was doing—to say he was having dinner with his grandfather, Nell casually asked around and discovered Kal was in a private room on the top floor of the hospital.

'It's all private rooms up there,' the young nurse added, with the kind of wonder usually reserved for talk of heaven.

Nell thanked her and departed, then was foiled as the

elevator wouldn't take her to that floor, needing a code of some kind to get her past the penultimate one.

She thought for a moment, remembering Kal's office had been on the top floor. She'd watched him key in some numbers and had thought nothing of it at the time, but now she closed her eyes and tried to recall his actions.

One seven zero nine—her birthday, now she thought about it. She smiled to herself as the elevator rose obediently up to that final floor, although it was hardly likely Kal had even set the code—and if he had, why choose *her* birthday?

A very officious-looking sister came towards her as she walked in what she assumed was the direction of the ward. Kal's office had been to the left and they certainly hadn't passed any private rooms, so she'd turned right along the corridor, pushing through some swing doors before seeing the woman.

'You are looking for someone?'

Nell held up the hospital ID she'd been given on her first day in the burns unit and the woman looked at it and frowned.

'We have none of your patients here,' she said.

'No, I'm here to see Dr al Kalada,' Nell told her, trying to sound just as officious herself.

But the woman wasn't swayed by officiousness. She frowned at Nell and said in tones of great disdain, 'He is seeing only family.'

At that moment a veiled woman in black robes, beneath which a lilac skirt peeped demurely, came out of a room further down the corridor. She said something and the sister turned away from Nell, answering then hurrying to do the woman's bidding.

Uncertain if it was one of the women who'd accompanied Kal's father into the ER, Nell moved forward hesi-
tantly. The woman watched her for a while, then ducked
back inside the room, returning a few seconds later with
a second black-robed figure. This woman came towards
Nell, her feet seeming to glide somehow above the floor
so smoothly did she move.

'You are Nell,' she said, holding out her hands and taking hold of Nell's in a warm clasp. 'Khalil is sleeping
now, but he has been worried about you and the boy. He
begs your forgiveness for not looking after the boy and
putting him in danger with the drive back to the city.'

The woman's face was masked, but her eyes, keen
with intelligence and so like Kal's she had to be his mother, were smiling anxiously at Nell.

'Patrick is fine,' she assured the woman. 'By now it
will seem a great adventure, and think how he'll be able
to boast about it to his friends when he returns to school.'

Wrong thing to say apparently, as the smile faded from
the warm brown eyes, which now looked puzzled.

But Nell felt tiredness wash over her. Perhaps relief
that Kal was all right might have caused it—or lack of
sleep the previous night from wondering how he was!
Whatever, she couldn't handle trying to figure out why
the woman now looked puzzled, so she asked if she could
see Kal, and was led into his room.

Five women sat around the bed, all quiet, although
three of them appeared to be praying. Only one wore the
trousers and tunic top that was the uniform of a nurse, so
the rest must be family. Nell glanced at the masked faces.
Was one of them his ex-wife? Would she still have the
right to sit by his bed?

Then his mother introduced them. This one was her sister, Kal's aunt, this one and this one sisters-in-law and the other his mother's friend, like an aunt but not so closely related. Nell said a weak hello to all of them, her mind more on the figure who lay motionless on the bed.

She looked at the nurse.

'He *is* sleeping?' she asked. 'It's not a coma? Have you done brain scans? It's not something worse than the recurrence of an old illness?'

The nurse beckoned her to come outside, then introduced herself. Her name was Annie, and she was English, working in the hospital because her husband worked here for one of the oil companies.

'I'm glad you got me out of there even if it's only for a short time,' she said. 'Yes, he's sleeping naturally. Last night he woke briefly and became so agitated the doctors put him into an induced coma, but just while they did brain scans and got his temperature down. At about eight this morning he came out of that and was alert. It *is* the old illness, nothing more sinister, but it's left him drained and he'll probably sleep for twenty-four hours.'

'But you're in there with him—he has a nurse with him all the time? Why, if he's OK?'

'The family!' Annie explained. 'You *do* know who they are? They're a bit like gods around here, they're so revered, so of course the doctor treating Dr al Kalada has insisted he have round-the-clock nursing care, although the doctor knows his relations will also stay with him. It's the custom here—but if you're the Australian doctor working in the burns unit, you already know that.'

She finished her explanation, then looked enquiringly at Nell.

'I guess you met him through the plane crash,' she said, but as far too many people in this hospital right now already knew of her relationship to Kal, Nell had no intention of explaining anything. She thanked the woman for the information and walked away, but as she made her way back down to the level where the bridge crossed to the apartments, she regretted not talking more to the English girl...

Anything would have been better than this sense of being very, very alone that she was experiencing right now...

CHAPTER TEN

PATRICK'S next phone call was to say he was back at the hospital, but as Kal was now awake he would call in and see him before coming back up to the apartment. And though she assured Patrick that would be all right, for the first time in her life she was jealous of him. That he would be able to see Kal and hear from his own lips that he was feeling better...

To see him with his eyes open, not deadly still and pale...

But to see him with all those people around? What could you say? Tell him you love him?

Yeah, right! And listen to another dissertation on the destructive elements of that particular emotional state...

Nell paced the room, passing and repassing the dinner she'd ordered, unable to eat as the depths of her anxiety about Kal tied her stomach into knots, while her mind began to wonder if perhaps what he was offering—a loveless marriage—would be better than not being with him at all.

No, half a loaf of bread might be better than no bread to a starving man, but hers was an emotional hunger, and she suspected it wouldn't be satisfied with half-measures.

She had made this decision—for about the hundredth time in the last few days—when a knock sounded on the door. Thinking it was Patrick, she strode towards it and flung it open. It wasn't Patrick but the small woman she had assumed was Kal's mother—accompanied by one of the other women, though Nell couldn't be sure which one.

'Patrick and my husband are with Khalil so I came to speak to you,' the woman said, her voice slightly hesitant but her English clear enough to be easily understood.

Nell ushered the pair inside and waved her hand towards the couch.

The two women sat, then Kal's mother pulled some sheets of paper from a pocket in her robes.

'We have one hundred and fourteen names on this already, and that is only what we have achieved today,' the woman said, handing the sheets of paper to Nell. 'I am sorry they are in Arabic but I do not write in English, but the names are there and already these ones have been registered, although the testing seems to take a little time.'

Nell looked at the pages with the graceful curves of Arabic script across them. They told her nothing and, try as she may to make sense of the conversation, nothing clicked.

'I don't understand,' she said softly, not wanting to offend this woman.

'Khalil told us last night about the boy's illness and the bone—bone marrow?—Patrick might need. He was disturbed he had not done something about it earlier and cursed his selfishness in wanting to get to know his son. He was so upset I assured him I would take care of it, so this is where we are now—the people on the list you have are all relatives, but by the end of the week my husband says we will have ten thousand more people on it, and more again the week after that. Khalil says he will get more specialists to do the tests so it does not take too long, and someone else to set up all the results on a computer. He says our country might become known as a donor bank—is "bank" the right word?—for all the world.'

Nell looked at the sheets of paper in her hand and shook her head. Last night this small robed woman who, Nell had no doubt, rarely ventured from her home had first heard of Patrick's plight, and now she was talking of a bank of thousands of would-be bone-marrow donors, all tested and listed there, ready to give something of themselves to save the life of a stranger.

'Thank you.' She said the words, but knew they were inadequate.

The woman waved away her thanks, then added, 'We pray that Patrick will not need it.' Her light brown eyes, so familiar to Nell, were soft with understanding. 'But I know why you had to come and ask us this thing, although it must have been a hard decision for you to make. Hard for you in your heart.'

Nell nodded, for that's where it *had* been hard—where it was hurting so much now.

They sat for a little while, Nell aware she should offer hospitality but too torn apart by conflicting emotions to find the necessary energy. Then the women rose, Kal's mother taking Nell's hands between hers and pressing them together.

'The road ahead might seem dark now, but it will lighten. I can see the glow of it ahead of you.'

Nell thanked her again, rising to her feet and following the two women to the door. She doubted anyone could see into the future, but the image of some glow ahead of her was a comforting one—though maybe the glow was the hot summer sun back in Australia, and somehow the thought of that glow wasn't nearly as enticing as it should be.

Kal was released from hospital the following day, and predictably Patrick begged to be allowed to accompany his father to the house in the family compound where he would convalesce for a few days.

'Well, I can hardly say no,' Nell said, a trifle tetchily. 'I can't expect you to hang around here all day on your own.'

Patrick ignored her mood, hugged and thanked her, then packed his bags and headed off, accompanied by a white-robed man who had been waiting in the corridor.

'This is Ahmed, one of Kal's men,' Patrick told her by way of introduction, then they left, Nell watching from the door of the apartment, more and more aware of the growing affection between her son and his father, and the growing attraction to Patrick of the life his father—or his father's family—led.

'So I bring him up, fight for his life, then lose him, not to cancer but to his father?'

The thought pained her so much she felt like crying, but she'd already shed her bucket of tears over Kal, and more than a bucket over the possibility of losing Patrick, so she refused to shed any more. She phoned home instead, speaking to both her parents, explaining why Patrick wasn't there to talk to them, telling them about the donor register getting under way, hearing their delight.

She had just hung up when the phone rang again.

'You didn't come to see me in hospital.'

Just hearing Kal's voice was enough to make her heart

thud erratically, but the accusation in his voice steeled her against any weakness.

'I came,' she said. 'You were asleep, and well protected against the wiles of casual women visitors.'

Kal laughed.

'Too well protected,' he said. 'I felt like a child again, living among the women. My father shooed them all out when he and Patrick visited.'

'Where's Patrick now?' Nell asked.

'He's out at the stables. Some of my younger cousins and their friends were playing soccer with him for a while, and now they're going riding. The trails are well lit and they know to keep a watch on him without him knowing it. They won't let him get too tired.'

Playing soccer, going riding, driving cars—what wasn't on offer for Patrick in his father's life?

There was a pause, then Kal said, 'It is ironic, isn't it, Nell, that you came here looking for insurance in the form of bone marrow in case it was needed to save Patrick's life, and it turns out he saved mine. Without prompt drug treatment, the encephalitis could have caused brain damage and even death.'

'Encephalitis?' Nell breathed, her grouchiness over Patrick's fun forgotten. 'You had encephalitis? No one mentioned that to me.'

'They didn't tell you?' Kal sounded puzzled. 'I thought my father—'

'Your father said it was a recurrence of something—I thought some minor virus—nasty and fast-acting, but encephalitis?'

'You should be careful, Nell.' His voice almost purred down the phone. 'You're sounding as if you care.'

'Of course I care,' Nell snapped at him. 'I've always cared. I love you, Kal. You're angry that I didn't tell you about Patrick. You feel denied and cheated. Well, I've done my penance for whatever wrong I might have done you—loving you has been my penance, and now look where that has led me.'

She slammed down the phone.

It rang again and, although she knew she shouldn't, she answered it.

'Where has it led you, Nell?' Kal asked, as if they hadn't been interrupted.

'It's led me to the point where we are now—the point you threatened me with—the point where Patrick gets to choose whether he stays with your fabulously wealthy and important family, where he gets to ride horses and probably camels and drive cars and go camping in the desert, or to go back home with dull old Mum. You've even got what will probably end up being the biggest bone-marrow donor register in the world happening, so you can use his health as an added enticement for him to stay. That's one that will play well in court.'

'Nell, stop! It needn't be like this. You must know I still have feelings for you, feelings that could well be love.'

'You wouldn't know love if it got up and bit you on the backside!'

She slammed the phone down again and left the apartment, not certain she'd be strong enough not to answer it a third time. She headed for the ward, then decided she hadn't the will to be as cheerful and positive as she needed to be for the patients she would see, so went down to the lobby instead. She'd been outside the hospital only once—the evening Kal had taken her and Patrick to dinner. She'd go for a walk. From what she remembered of the drive to the hotel, there were parks spread through the city like emerald-green oases.

'Taxi?'

The cab edged up behind her as she came out the front doors, and suddenly she had a better idea.

'Could you drive me out to the desert?' she asked.

The driver looked puzzled. Maybe he didn't understand English.

'To the desert? You want to drive out to the desert?'

His English was OK, he just didn't understand the request.

Nell smiled at him.

'I've been here for nearly two weeks and I keep hearing about the desert, but I haven't seen it. Would you drive me out there—it needn't be too far—then wait for me while I look at it for a while?'

'It is night-time, lady,' the driver said, no doubt sure she was mad.

'But there's a moon,' she pointed out. Then she opened her handbag and counted out how much she had in local currency. Patrick had got her some from an automatic teller machine on his first day in town when he'd asked for some change and she'd realised she hadn't any money. Now she offered the man her collection of notes.

'Would this be enough?'

'To drive you to the desert and wait there for you? It is far too much.'

He named a sum and, although he continued to shake his head, he allowed her to climb into the back of the cab, and he took off slowly out of the hospital grounds, speeding up as they reached the main road, but still driving carefully, as if he needed to be fully alert should his passenger show further signs of derangement.

Eventually they left the city and drove along a wide highway, lined on either side with what Nell assumed were date palms. She was reasonably sure the darkness beyond the palms was desert, but the driver seemed to understand she needed something more. Eventually he turned off the highway, drove a little way, then stopped.

'My car is not made to cross the sand,' he said, turning in his seat to look at her. 'But up ahead is the first of the sandhills that run east-west across the country. If you walk up there, you will see them ranging into the distance, though not as well, of course, as if you'd come during the day.'

'Night is fine,' Nell told him, but didn't add that night was what she needed, because night would hide the tears she knew she'd probably shed.

'I will leave the headlights on so you can see the way and find the way back, and, lady, please, do not go beyond my headlights, or I will get very worried about you.'

'I won't leave the lights, and thank you,' Nell said, then she opened the car door and got out, slipping off her shoes so she could feel the texture of the sand beneath her feet, her mind a muddle of so many things that for a while she was content not to think at all.

The warm night air wrapped around her, a slight breeze lifting her hair and brushing against her skin. After that first time, she and Kal had often camped at South Stradbroke, walking across to the dunes at night, finding a special magic in the sand and sea and moonlight.

And if ever she'd needed magic, it was now. Kal's mother saw a glow in her future—a glow from the fiery conflagration that would be her fight with Kal, because no way would she let her son go easily.

Even if life here would be better for him? Not only financially, but in every way? Not even if he chose to live with his father?

Nell crossed her arms across her chest as if the action might stop her heart from bursting. Who was she kidding? As if she could ever put Patrick through the emotional agony of making a choice between her and Kal.

Knowing Patrick, she knew he wouldn't stay without her blessing, but his choice, given one, would be to have her stay, too. And being Patrick, he'd make sure Nell's parents were included in whatever arrangements were made—Kal would probably send the jet over to bring them to visit whenever they wished!

The bitterness of that last thought made her shiver. She'd think about Patrick's likely first choice—her staying on.

She'd reached the top of the dune and sat down, not so much to look out over the desert as to consider her future.

She'd have a job—Yasmeen had said they'd been advertising for a specialist to head the burns unit, without success.

But there'd be Kal…

'Nell.'

No wonder the taxi driver thought I was mad. Now I'm hearing voices.

'Nell, I'm coming up the sand hill now. I didn't want to startle you.'

Nell turned in disbelief.

'Are you having me followed?' she demanded. 'And what do you think you're doing here when you're just out of hospital? Have you no sense at all? How do you think

Patrick would feel to find his father, then have him drop dead because he didn't look after himself?'

Kal reached her side and dropped to sit beside her.

'Stupid, I know, but I didn't drive. Ahmed brought me. Well, he took me to the hospital and I saw you getting into a cab and I did that "follow that car" thing for the first time in my life, then when we stopped beside the cab, the driver seemed prepared to defend you to the death until Ahmed and I managed to persuade him it was a lovers' tryst. I told him who I was, and eventually he agreed to drive back to town.'

'You sent my cab away?' Nell knew this wasn't the point she should be arguing but it seemed a stable point she could latch onto in the morass of her emotions.

'But I hadn't paid him.'

Kal laughed and moved a little closer, putting his arm around her shoulders and giving her a little hug.

'I paid him,' he assured her, but although that issue was settled, something else had occurred to Nell. She moved away from Kal's arm so she could make the point more decisively.

'And it's definitely not a lovers' tryst!'

'It could be,' Kal murmured, but he didn't touch her again. Instead, he drew up his knees and rested his chin on them, looking out over the rolling sands of the desert.

'Did you think of the island when you came here?' he asked.

Nell nodded, unable to lie about memories that were so precious to her.

'I, too, think about it whenever I am in the desert. Maybe that's why I spend all my days off out here, usually alone, though sometimes with my birds for company.'

He was silent for a long time, then he spoke again.

'Do you think that's love, Nell? Fourteen years of coming to the desert to sit on a dune like this and think about the island? To think about you?'

Nell couldn't speak. Her throat had closed up so tightly she felt she might never speak again. And Kal didn't seem to need an answer, though he moved slightly and rested one hand lightly on her shoulder.

'I can hear your laugh when I'm out here,' he continued quietly. 'In the city there's too much noise to hear it, but out here I see you running down the sand hills, laughing at the sky, and I can hear the joyous sound of it. Is that love, Nell?'

Nell shrugged, not to move his hand but in answer to his question. She had never been able to return to the island, afraid memories would overwhelm her there, but if Kal really did come out here and think of her—was it love?

'I thought it was obsession.' His words hovered in the air. 'A kind of madness I should be able to shake off. "Physician, cure thyself"—that's what I used to quote, but there was no cure, and that was bad. I am not a man who should have obsessions. Then one day you were there, bent over a dead man in a disaster zone, calmly taking charge, turning to me and saying, "Hello, Kal," as if we'd parted yesterday.'

His hand grew heavy on her shoulder, but Nell knew he hadn't finished, while in herself she wanted to be sure she was more than an obsession.

Would he get to that?

'So that was bad enough, then you sprang Patrick on me, and although I knew in some part of my mind you'd acted in what you saw as my best interests at the time, I was angry, Nell, so angry, yet bereft as well, with grief that I had lost all those years of my son's life. Can you understand that?'

This time Nell nodded, although Kal was still looking out across the desert, not at her.

'But even though I blamed you, I needed you. I looked for you and sought you out and felt better being near you, even when we were fighting all the time.'

He turned towards her now, and lifted his hand to move her chin so she was facing him.

'Is that love, Nell? Does love hurt when you are arguing with the object of that love? Does it make us lash out to hurt the loved one in return? I can't believe it can be, Nell. I can't believe if I really loved you I would threaten to take away your son. Is love so irrational? Is it so confusing we do wrong in its name?'

Nell stared at him, seeing his familiar face, made young by moonlight, in this unfamiliar setting.

'I don't think love's about hurting people, Kal, but neither can it protect anyone from hurt. Love's about being there for each other when hurt happens—that's when love is needed, sharing the hurt as well as the joy. It's like the desert, stretching endlessly to the horizon—limitless. As hard to quantify as the grains of sand we're sitting on.'

She turned away, looking out over the play of moonlight on the rolling sand hills.

'Can I apply for the job as head of the burns unit?'

'You'll stay?'

The joy in his voice was unmistakable.

Pity she had to kill it...

'If Patrick decides he'd like to live here then, yes, I'd like to get a job so I can be near him. That's what I came out to the desert to decide. What would be best for Patrick. I won't fight you over him, Kal, or have him made to choose between us. He's been through enough lately and doesn't need that kind of pressure from people who supposedly love him.'

'But you'd stay with me! We'd be a family! Of course you can work if you want to. We couldn't hope for a more qualified surgeon to head the unit, but you talk as if—'

'As if we'd be apart? Wouldn't we, Kal? Even if we shared a house, for form's sake or for Patrick's or your family's, wouldn't we still be apart?'

'You don't believe I love you.'

The statement fell between them, flat and somehow ugly.

'How can I, Kal, when you're still not sure yourself? When you still think of me as an obsession, and look hopefully for a cure. We could share a house, even share a bed, and, yes, that part would be good, but inside I'd be dying, Kal. If that sounds dramatic, I'm sorry. But love can't live in a vacuum. It needs to be nurtured, not with gifts and promises but with love returned.'

He stood up and walked away, down the sloping face of the sand hill—not towards the car but away from it.

Then he turned and raised his arms towards the night sky.

'What do we do when words are not enough?' he said, asking not her but the stars and moon. 'Here we see the magnitude of nature, but how to show the magnitude of love?'

He turned around, the white robe whirling around his body, then he walked back towards her and knelt in front of her.

'Yes, it's an obsession, but I don't want a cure, Nell.

Because it's love as well. A love so deep and strong and all-consuming you might call it an obsession. But however it's labelled, I hope it will remain with me for the rest of my life.' He took her hands and lifted them to his lips.

'As I hope you will remain with me for the rest of my life…'

Her heart tap-tapping against her rib cage and hope tap-tapping in her head, Nell spoke his name, knowing her uncertainty and disbelief would be echoing through the word.

'Kal?'

He drew her closer, and silenced any further questions with the lightest of butterfly kisses.

'I love you, Nell,' he said, his voice gravely deep—desperately sincere.

'I was really sure all along. Right from when I saw you again at the airport,' he added quietly. 'But some stubborn streak kept getting in the way of admitting it. Yet the more I denied love, and derided it, the more certain I was inside that it was what I felt for you.'

He cupped her face in his hands and looked deep into her eyes.

'I'm a man who is used to being in control,' he said, 'but with you I lose it completely, and that's a very scary thing for an al Kalada.'

'So you'll stay scared for as long as we're together?' Nell teased, high on happiness now she was certain that the miracle of love had embraced her once again. Embraced her and Kal and, within that magic circle, Patrick.

'I imagine so,' Kal said gloomily.

'Well, that's good,' Nell told him. 'Because one of the

good things about love is that you can hold tight to each other when you're scared.'

She moved closer and kissed him on the lips, then held him very tightly indeed.

HARLEQUIN *Presents*

Passion and Seduction Guaranteed!

She's sexy, successful and pregnant!

Relax and enjoy our fabulous series about couples whose passion results in pregnancies... sometimes unexpected!

Share the surprises, emotions, drama and suspense as our parents-to-be come to terms with the prospect of bringing a new life into the world. All will discover that the business of making babies brings with it the most special joy of all....

February's Arrival:

PREGNANT BY THE MILLIONAIRE

by Carole Mortimer

What happens when Hebe Johnson finds out she's pregnant with her noncommittal boss's baby?

Find out when you buy your copy of this title today!

REQUEST YOUR FREE BOOKS!

2 FREE NOVELS
PLUS 2
FREE GIFTS!

YES! Please send me 2 FREE Harlequin Presents® novels and my 2 FREE gifts. After receiving them, if I don't wish to receive any more books, I can return the shipping statement marked "cancel." If I don't cancel, I will receive 6 brand-new novels every month and be billed just $3.80 per book in the U.S., or $4.47 per book in Canada, plus 25¢ shipping and handling per book and applicable taxes, if any*. That's a savings of close to 15% off the cover price! I understand that accepting the 2 free books and gifts places me under no obligation to buy anything. I can always return a shipment and cancel at any time. Even if I never buy another book from Harlequin, the two free books and gifts are mine to keep forever.

106 HDN EEXK   306 HDN EEXV

Name _____ (PLEASE PRINT)

Address _____ Apt. #

City _____ State/Prov. _____ Zip/Postal Code

Signature (if under 18, a parent or guardian must sign)

Mail to the **Harlequin Reader Service®:**
IN U.S.A.: P.O. Box 1867, Buffalo, NY 14240-1867
IN CANADA: P.O. Box 609, Fort Erie, Ontario L2A 5X3

Not valid to current Harlequin Presents subscribers.

Want to try two free books from another line?
Call 1-800-873-8635 or visit www.morefreebooks.com.

* Terms and prices subject to change without notice. NY residents add applicable sales tax. Canadian residents will be charged applicable provincial taxes and GST. This offer is limited to one order per household. All orders subject to approval. Credit or debit balances in a customer's account(s) may be offset by any other outstanding balance owed by or to the customer. Please allow 4 to 6 weeks for delivery.

Your Privacy: Harlequin is committed to protecting your privacy. Our Privacy Policy is available online at www.eHarlequin.com or upon request from the Reader Service. From time to time we make our lists of customers available to reputable firms who may have a product or service of interest to you. If you would prefer we not share your name and address, please check here. ☐